THE BAD GIRL

ASHLEY ROSE

Thanks to Amy Truppi

Yamashiro's
The night air is crisp and fresh on my bare arms as Hunter leads me by the hand down to the bonsai garden on the hillside below the Japanese restaurant

Perched high above Los Angeles, the Japanese restaurant offers a spectacular view of the city lights below. I've never seen L.A. from this vantage point and it takes my breath away. Small fairy lights dot the edge of the path through a bonsai garden. We are alone.

My mom and Oscar are at the bar at the restaurant above us. We've just had a magical dinner to celebrate my high school graduation. My mom had offered to throw me a big party, but I'm a little burned out on parties.

The past week had been parties all the time:

Hunter and his stepsister, my close friend, Paige had a giant joint party in their massive backyard. It seemed like hundreds of people had attended. I'd actually skipped out of that one early. It was all movie people that Hunter's dad worked with in Hollywood. I recognized several movie stars. I felt like a hick in my white sundress. Not the first time I'd felt this way in L.A.

I barely saw Hunter. Or Paige. They had to smile and shake hands and visit all night. Hunter's father ordered him to "circulate" from table to table.

It was their job, his dad had told Paige and Hunter, pointing out that everyone who showed up had probably brought each of them a card and check for at least a hundred dollars, if not much more. With that guilt trip, Hunter had given me a long kiss at the door.

"You sure you have to go?" he'd asked. I eyed him. He looked hot in his black blazer.

I wish we could sneak off to his room above the garage.

"Yeah, baby. You're going to be busy," I'd said.

He'd nodded.

But before I left, I sent him a text as he walked away and waited for him to read it.

"I'm so hot for you. That blazer turns me on."

I could see when the text went through because he grabbed his phone, looked down, and then stopped walking. Then he turned around and gave me a scowl.

Then he texted back. "Not fair."

I gave him a sweet wave and left.

Then Coral's graduation party was even more insane as far as rich people and celebrities and setting. Her parents had rented a room at the J. Paul Getty museum. At least that party was more fun. Our friend group sat at one of the twenty or so big round tables. We secretly poured shots from a flask into our sodas under the table. Coral did have to do the obligatory stopping to chat at each table, but it was more organized and easier so she also got time to sit and talk to us.

Emma and the twins, Dex and Devin, had normal parties, where you go to their house and there's pulled pork sandwiches and chips and sodas in the backyard.

I didn't want any of this. And I was way burned out on parties. So, dinner for four it was.

Now, looking out over the lights of L.A. I remember something that happened after dinner that is still bothering me.

The dinner itself was amazing. Yamashiro's is a candlelit and magical place that makes you feel like you've been picked up and dropped in Japan. The food is also delicious and when we are done eating, Oscar and my mom say they want to grab another drink at the bar. My mom is talking to Oscar about her new job and her plans to eventually start her own accounting agency so she can work at home or wherever she wants.

Hunter and I decide to go check out the bonsai garden. We start to head outside but Hunter wants to swing by the bathroom. But I remember I left my sweater on the back of my chair. Hunter offers to get it but I tell him I'll grab it while he uses the bathroom. As I walk back to retrieve it, I pass the bar and hear my mom say my dad's name.

I draw up short. Then I hear the word "appeal."

A year ago, my mom and I were living in fear of my violent, abusive dad. Then he beat her so bad she ended up in the hospital and he landed in prison for seven years. Now they are officially divorced and we have a whole new life in California.

I will never forgive him. I don't ever want to see him or talk to him again.

A few weeks ago, my mom received a letter from him where he claimed to be sober and wanted her to forgive him. She had planned on flying out to visit him but then got her new job and the trip was postponed. At the time, she told me that I should consider forgiving my dad. Not for him. But for me. So, my hatred and resentment didn't eat me up inside.

I told her I was just fine.

But now a cold chill runs over me. She said the word "appeal."

"What?" I am suddenly beside them. "Is dad trying to get an appeal?"

My mom actually jumps. "I thought you and Hunter were outside."

"What about dad?"

Oscar looks down. *Oh fuck*, I think.

"It's nothing. At least right now. We can talk about it another night, right, honey?" my mom says.

Before I can argue, Hunter is at my side holding my sweater. "Ready?"

He'd seen me talking and grabbed it already. I look from my mom's face to Oscar's and know they aren't going to talk to me right then no matter what, so I nod and leave with Hunter.

He leads me through the bonsai garden path until we get to the bottom. Below us is brush and steep terrain. Before us is the whole of Los Angeles at night. He wraps me in his arms, hugging me from behind as we both stare at the city lights below—blue and red and yellow fairy lights sprinkled for as far as the eye can see.

"How you doin', Boots?" He asks me now.

I debate whether to tell him what I'm afraid to even say out loud: that my mom uttered my dad's name and the word "appeal" in the same breath.

I think about it for a few seconds before answering. I can't go there. I need to focus on what's right here before me. My boyfriend and my wonderful new life. I tell him this.

"I'm just feeling really grateful —for you, my mom's new life, living with Oscar, our friend group—but I'm also both excited and terrified of what the future holds."

He gives me a squeeze and whispers in my ear. "Me, too."

I turn in his arms. "Really?"

He nods, looking down at me. "I'm excited to go to Mexico and shed light on what's going on there, but I don't want to be away from you that long," he says.

Hunter received a Fulbright scholarship that will pay for him to travel to the slums of Mexico for six months to film a documentary on children taking up arms to protect their village from the cartel.

"I'm jealous," I say. "If I were in your shoes, I wouldn't hesitate for a second."

"I'm not hesitating," he says and pause. "I just don't want things to change while I'm gone."

I nod. "I know."

"I don't want you to ... not feel the same way when I get back. Six months is a long time," he says.

"I can't imagine not feeling the same way, Hunter West," I say looking up at his eyes in the near dark. "I'm crazy about you."

He leans down and his mouth is inches from mine. I reach for his head and pull him even closer, my fingers becoming tangled in his hair. His mouth is white hot on mine and there is an urgency and fierceness in his kiss that suddenly makes me desperate for him.

As his mouth travels, down to my neck and he buries his face in my hair and shoulder, his hands grab my hips and pull me so close it feels like every inch of us from chest to feet is pressed together.

I want him more than ever before.

It's an unfamiliar desperation, I've never felt.

His fingers are under the straps of my sundress and effortlessly pull the dress down to my waist and then his mouth is on me, hot and wet on my nipples and I'm panting with desire, my hands buried deep in his hair pulling him closer to me.

Suddenly, he moves even lower and my dress is on the ground and he has tugged on my panties so his mouth can get to me. Now my fingers are deep in his hair as I frantically pull him closer begging him not to stop.

I'm gasping and clutching at him unaware of anything now except the intense circles of pleasure that pulse through me and seem like they are never going to end. When they do, Hunter stands and effortlessly lifts me up so that my legs are wrapped around him and he shifts and enters me so deeply that the circles continue like aftershocks, nearly as strong.

He comes quickly and forcefully and gently sets me back down. The world slowly comes into focus again. We are standing in the dark of a bonsai garden that overlooks the city of Los Angeles. Hunter gently hands me my dress and I slip it back on. I don't know where my panties are in the dark.

I've just had the best orgasm of my life. And it was in public. Where anyone could have stumbled upon us. And just as I think this, we hear voices at the top of the garden where the path begins. We hurriedly pull apart from one another.

"Jesus," he says in a husky whisper in my ear. We are both

breathing heavy but manage to appear composed by the time an older couple turns the corner and comes across us. Although I still don't know where my underwear is. But it's too late to look for them now.

We smile and walk past, holding hands, back up to the restaurant where Oscar and my mom are waiting.

2

Back at my house, I change out of my petal pink sundress and throw on my cutoff levis and my faded and soft Brooklyn T-shirt and head downstairs. Hunter has changed in the downstairs bathroom into board shorts and a tight black T-shirt.

My mom and Oscar are about to head out on the deck with glasses of wine when we say goodbye.

"Off to Part Two?" My mom asks, smiling. I nod. But I also think that whatever she was saying about my dad is not good. I'm almost afraid to find out and a little relieved I'll put off knowing a little longer. Ignorance is bliss.

When she says part two, she means the second half of my graduation party night that involves meeting our friends at the beach. But I'm also wondering if it might mean part two with Hunter. Our sex in the bonsai garden has only made me want him again as soon as possible.

But right now, we are meeting friends.

When we arrive at Balboa Beach, everyone is already there. They have a small bonfire staked out already and someone brought beach chairs. We sit surrounding the fire and pass around a bottle of vodka to spike our sodas.

Coral stands and sets up a portable speaker and then turns to us. "I made a playlist of all the songs that we loved and listened to together as friends during our senior year," she says.

"Bitch, you are going to make me cry for sure tonight, aren't you?" Paige says.

"That's the plan," Coral says.

Emma laughs.

I look over at her and want to cry.

Emma is going to be the first of us to leave.

Tomorrow her dad is driving her to the airport so she can fly to Germany where she was accepted to a summer program as an English language teacher.

Paige isn't far behind. Mid-summer she leaves for Stanford. She got hired as a research assistant at the school, so she'll move and start working before school starts in the fall.

Coral and Dex and Devin have all decided to go to school in Southern California at various schools so I'll still be able to see them.

Hunter doesn't leave for Mexico until late August. I'm more nervous about his work in close proximity to the Mexican cartel than what it might do to our relationship.

But we are going to be able to see each other all summer since we are both working on his dad's movie set.

My big break earlier this year was to impress the hell out of Hunter's dad, Brock West, a few weeks ago when a film Hunter and I made won an honorable mention at a film festival. He offered me an internship on his movie set this summer.

And Hunter had already planned on working for his dad all summer.

Besides having insane chemistry together, Hunter and I also share a passion for filmmaking.

When my mom made me move to L.A. last summer, I had no idea what awaited me. I didn't know that I would grow to love my friend group so deeply that even the thought of some of us moving away was breaking my heart in two.

Sure enough, Coral's play list had all us girls weeping and Dex and Devin and Hunter swearing and pissed off.

"This is such a cheap shot," Devin says. "Is your goal to make us cry? No, really? I don't cry in front of girls."

"But you cry?" Emma says.

"Maybe. What's it to you."

"He cries like a baby," his twin brother, Dex says, with his arm loped around Coral. "All you gotta do is play the movie *Up* and he's a big weeping crybaby."

"So?" Devin says laughing. "I'm man enough to own it. But I don't want to cry tonight. Is there something wrong with that?"

But then Coral puts on Juice Wrld's song about him dying young and the guys say, "Fuck that," and take off toward the water.

It is a sad song that seems to predict his death at 21.

"He was my favorite," Emma says, wiping away her tears.

"Dex's too," Coral says, looking over to where the guys are standing near where the waves are breaking.

"I'm going to miss all of you so much," Emma says.

Big group hug and then we dry tears and tell funny stories. The guys come back.

In the distance, I can see another group gathered around a bonfire and wonder if it's other students from Pacific High. This is our stretch of beach and while other people definitely come here, it seems like we come here the most.

Then a group heads our way. As they grow closer, my heart races.

I've only been here a year, but I have enemies.

People who hate me badly enough to hurt me if they have the chance—emotionally, physically, mentally—any way they can.

Josh Masters tried to rape me. A girl we go to school with, Ava, doctored a video tape of that night so it appeared it was consensual, the judge dropped the charges. And because Josh was kicked off the football team, most of the team, which had its worst season ever, still hates me.

So, when the group strolls by our bonfire, I'm holding my breath, hoping it's not anyone who wants to ruin the last night our friend group is together.

They walk by without stopping or commenting and I let out my breath.

We continue to drink and tell stories and laugh until we cry and don't leave until the flames grow low and all that is left are embers.

Before we leave, we all stand in the parking lot under the harsh halogen lights.

Suddenly, nobody has anything to say.

"Well," Devin finally says. "I guess this is it, Emma."

He walks over and wraps her in his arms and then we are all in a huge group hug.

Hunter drives me home. I'm quiet the entire way.

He walks me to the door and wraps me in his arm. The intense desire I felt earlier in the night is gone, now I'm just sleepy and weepy and want to tug on my fuzziest pajamas and crawl in bed.

Hunter holds me and hugs me and kisses me sweetly on the forehead.

I open the front door.

Before he walks away he says, "You okay, Boots?"

I nod in the dark as I walk into the house. I'm afraid if I speak I'll cry.

3

The next morning I'm still in my flannel pajama pants and soft tee-shirt I sleep in when I go downstairs.

All night I've been tossing and turning thinking about my dad and what I overheard last night.

And I woke remembering that earlier this year, I'd made a vow to start tackling all of my deepest fears one by one. It started with riding a roller coaster:

I don't eat breakfast or lunch. I'm too nervous about riding a roller coaster later.

When Hunter picks me up he has the biggest grin.

"What?" I say.

"This is awesome. I'm going to start calling you Roller Coaster Girl."

"Please don't."

When we get to the Santa Monica Pier, I almost turn around and run back to the car. My hands are shaking. What the hell? It's such a stupid thing to be afraid of.

And then, standing at the foot of it and looking up it hits me. I know why I'm afraid. I'm suddenly a toddler again at Casino Pier in New Jersey. I'm holding my dad's hand and he's looking up at the roller coaster. And then suddenly he lets go of my hand and is gone.

I look around the crowd, frantic, but I don't see my dad. I'm scared and start to cry.

Then he's back at my side and holding me. "Pumpkin, it's okay. I'm so sorry. I saw something—someone doing something dangerous and I had to go help. I'm so sorry if you were scared."

He scoops me up in his arms and I cry even harder.

And just like that with this memory I want to cry.

For one, it's the dad of my childhood, the dad I loved and looked up to so much. And then it's also the realization that it's not the roller coaster I'm afraid of. It's just that I was afraid and now I've somehow associated that with the ride.

Hunter nudges me. "Hey? You good?"

I turn and smile at him. "I'm great. Let's do this."

"That's my girl," he says.

"Give me just one second," I say at the last minute and lean on the rail overlooking the water. Remembering my dad like this, hits hard.

I suddenly realize that there is another thing on my list: I'm afraid of my dad. I'm afraid to see him. I'm afraid to trust him. I'm afraid to love him again. Because I'm afraid he will hurt me. Not physically, but emotionally.

That might be my biggest fear—above everything else. I close my eyes and with the heat of the sun on my face, realize that confronting my dad is going to be added to my list. And that I'm going to cross it off.

I rode that roller coaster like a boss. And I know I will figure out how to hear my dad's name without going into a tailspin.

I march right down to my mom's bedroom and knock.

She opens her bedroom door. She's already showered and dressed for work. She's putting on her earrings and smiles when she sees me.

"Did you have fun last night?"

I smile and nod. "Yes, thanks. Yamashiro's was magical." *In more ways than one.*

"It really was, wasn't it?"

"Mom," I say and swallow down my reluctance.

"Honey. I didn't want to upset you at your party," she says. "Your dad is trying to appeal his sentence."

"Based on what?"

My mom sighs. "The appeal is based on some obscure legal technicality with the jury."

"Is he getting out of prison?" I say, fear racing through me.

She shrugs and reaches for her blazer. I follow her as she starts up the stairs to the main floor.

"I don't know."

"Are you worried?" I ask her. *Are you scared?*

Turning, she flashes me a brilliant smile. "Not one single bit. I told you I was going to go visit him. He's better now, Kennedy. When he's not drinking he's a very nice person. And he's been sober for a while now. I know we haven't seen that side of him for a long time, but it's still there."

"Are you sure?"

"Yes," she says and leans over to kiss my cheek. "Have a good day. I have to go."

As she walks out, I think, *but what if he starts drinking again?*

There are good memories. When my mom says he's nice, I can grab ahold of a few memories that make this true.

In some ways, I'm still the little girl who used to spend Sunday mornings sitting by his side as he did crossword puzzles in the paper and try to help him figure out the answers. The little girl who used to drag him off the couch to play catch on Saturday afternoons. Or the little girl he would take on a weekly date to the ice cream shop.

But that man I loved eventually disappeared—was swallowed up by the man who loved alcohol more than anything else in his life, including his family. But deep inside I still remember the dad he was when I was young.

When I was little...before...my dad would always be there to play catch with me or take me to a matinee. He was a more involved dad than most of my friend's dads who were big Wall Street guys. My dad was a firefighter so he was home for days at a time. And he liked to spend them with me.

Once, right before things went bad, I had a terrible time at school. I got a period stain on my pants in junior high and didn't know it until I got home. I was mortified, certain that the entire school had seen it.

I told my mom and she told my dad. The next morning, I refused to go to school. Instead of my mom coming in to talk to me about it, my dad did. The last person a 12-year-old girl wants to talk to about her period. But my dad was very matter-of-face. He sat down and told me a story about pooping his pants in high school. He and his friends had gone to this crazy spicy Mexican food restaurant and while he was in class he thought he'd farted. And it began to smell. He ran out of class, but not soon enough.

The next day he walked down the hall at school with his head held high and any time anyone said something to him—which they did—he smiled and said, "That's right motherfucker."

When he told me this, I rolled my eyes. It wasn't the same. It was totally different. I wasn't a guy and I wasn't going to tell anyone to eff off.

But I did hold my head high the next day. And it worked.

My dad was a good dad. Until his mom died and he started drinking, lost his job, and got violent with my mom.

The first time it happened, I heard my mom crying and yelling at him that he was going to be just like his dad. I'd never met my grandfather. My grandmother had divorced him when my dad was probably eight years old. In those days, that was really rare, I now know.

I miss that dad. But he died in my mind a long time ago. After nanna died, I never saw that dad again.

Hunter and I spend the rest of the week at the beach.

We load the car with blankets and coolers of drinks and snacks and books and portable speakers.

Each morning, we stake out the same spot and spend the day lying in the sun, splashing in the waves or bodysurfing or playing volleyball. Friends and people we know come and go. This is our last true week of summer vacation, maybe forever.

On Monday, we start working full time on the movie set. And after that, I start college and then will probably always have jobs during the summer until I have a full-time job in my career.

Every moment feels precious and fragile.

Throughout the day at the beach, every once in a while, I peek over at Hunter's lean, long-limbed bronze body and wonder how I ever got a boy who looks like that to be all mine. There are moments like this when I am still astounded. I only had one boyfriend before that, a very sweet nerdy guy named Ryan who was my best friend but who never set my body on fire.

It wasn't until Hunter kissed me for the first time that I truly knew what lust really was. And forgot about my decision to remain a virgin until college. Now I can't get enough of him. I never knew I had it in me until this boy's mouth touched mine.

One day, when the sun has already set and the beach has started to empty, I roll over on top of his warm back. I mold myself to his back and kiss the side of his neck. Then in one swift move, I untie my bikini top, pull it out from under me and press my bare breasts against his back. He groans and the wriggles underneath me until he's on his back.

"Kennedy," he moans. "We can't. Not here."

I lift my head and look around. "There's nobody around for miles."

"So, you say."

And as the sun disappears, I kiss him until his protests end and we make love in the dark on the beach.

At one point, he reaches for a towel and tries to drape it over us, but it quickly falls to one side and for a few intense and urgent moments, we forget the entire world.

Having sex in a public place is exciting. I think I'm getting addicted to it.

But more than that, I'm addicted to Hunter. Everything about him. Even if we never have sex again and just hold hands, I would still want to be with him.

If only our summer could go on like this forever, I think as we drive home.

But at the same time, I'm super excited to be an intern on a high budget movie set working with some of the most talented people in the business. And I get to see Hunter every day on the set.

We start Monday and I'm looking forward to it.

I spend the weekend with my mom and Oscar and trying to figure out how to dress on a movie set. My mom and I are living with Oscar until she makes enough money at her new job for us to move out. But Oscar doesn't want us to hurry. He says he loves the company. I love him and love living in a gorgeous beach house in Malibu.

I keep texting Hunter about my wardrobe dilemma, and he thinks it's hilarious.

"Anything you own is fine," he says.

"What? Like my cutoff jeans and crop top."

"Not that, goof," he says. "Just wear pants and a shirt and you'll be fine."

"That is not helpful," I say. "Dressy? Casual?"

"Boots, I don't know," he finally says in exasperation.

Oscar, my mom's best friend, is not only gay but he also works on films as a director of photography. In fact, he's the director of photography on the same movie. So, he should be of help. You'd think.

"Just wear something you feel comfortable in," he says.

"I feel comfortable in my fuzzy slippers and flannel pajama pants, but somehow don't think that's what you mean," I say.

He's making us tacos in the kitchen with cilantro crème sauce. He turns to me and rolls his eyes.

"Okay. You want to look casual but professional, right?"

"Yes!" I say pulling out a bar stool and getting excited. Finally, somebody is going to tell me how to dress!

"What do you have that fits that description?" he asks.

My excitement disappears. "I don't know."

I wear miniskirts, sexy sweet sundresses, crop tops, and ripped jeans. Nothing that would fit his description.

"Oscar," I say feeling desperation creep into my voice. "You just gotta dress me. I'm serious. You have to tell me what to wear? Please?"

He finally takes me serious. "Okay, that's all you had to say. I got this."

"You do?"

"Yeah," he grabs his phone and taps and after a few minutes takes out his credit card and hands me his phone. "Go to the mall and buy an outfit that makes you look exactly like this."

I take the phone from him. It's a young woman in slim black trousers, a button down black blouse with the sleeves rolled up and black ballet flats.

"This?" I ask frowning.

"Yep."

I frown.

"Kennedy, you asked. Are you going to listen to me or not?

"Fine, but I'll look like I'm going to a funeral."

"Whoa," he says. "When you first moved here, all you wore was black."

"I've evolved," I say snarkily and then bust out laughing. 'Plus, black is how you dress if you live in Brooklyn."

He laughs too. "Just try this for the first day. If it feels uncomfortable or you see other people dressing differently, you can adjust, but this is a great way to not stick out your first day."

I'm still feeling snarky so I say, "Maybe I want to stick out."

"Nope. Not your first day. You are there to work and learn and help Brock West, right?"

Brock West. Director extraordinaire. Intimidating as hell. Hunter's dad.

"Yes."

"Then dress the way I say."

"Okay. Fine."

I walk away without the credit card.

"Kennedy?" he says and holds it up.

"It's okay. My mom has some money now."

Oscar has spent the past year supporting me. Ever since I moved here. And now that my mom is working as an accountant she does have money to give me for clothes. I can go to Ross or some discount clothing store. The outfit Oscar pointed out should be easy to find and pretty affordable. I can even look for a Target or something.

"Please allow me to buy these items for you as a graduation present," he says.

"Oscar, you already bought your friend's minivan for me," I say, scrunching up my face. I'd been driving the minivan most of the year while his friend was out of the country. When his friend asked if we wanted to buy it, Oscar bought it for me.

Oscar is my mom's oldest friend. Her family took him in when they were teenagers when he got kicked out of the house for being gay. When my dad beat my mom up and was sent to prison while she was still recovering form her injures, Oscar took me in. He's like a second dad.

I know I'll forever be grateful to Oscar for saving our lives and don't want to take any more of his money.

But the look he gives me. I nod.

"Okay. Thanks," I say in a quiet voice.

"And don't go to Forever 21. You're going to want quality items. Go to Nordstrom and pick out the best quality, best fitting black shirt and pants and shoes you can find. And get three exact same outfits. Got it? This outfit can come in handy for the next few years, okay?"

I reluctantly agree.

Monday, I follow Oscar's pink Hummer as he drives to the movie set. Oscar said we should drive separate cars because we could have different hours. I'm sipping my coffee as I drive with the moon in front of me and wondering why on earth I ever agreed to intern for a job that requires me to get up in the middle of the night.

Our call is for five, which means I have to leave the house at 4:30. Insane.

And what's even more insane is that the freeway is busy. Where in the hell are all these people going at this hour?

Once we exit off the freeway in Los Angeles, Oscar slows down to keep me right behind him. Soon we are at the movie studio gate. It doesn't look like much. A gate surrounding a massive compound of gray walls.

Inside, the movie lot is like a small village of warehouses. We wind down narrow rounds until he shows me where to park: in an area marked crew parking. By now the sky in the east is starting to show pink.

"You hungry?" he asks as we walk by a food truck. People are lined up in front of it. I spot an actor I recognize from a sitcom I love. I try not to stare.

I shake my head. I'm too nervous to eat.

"You can order anything you want each day. It's part of the production costs. We feed you."

I nod.

"I'll take you to Brock West's office first," he says.

I'm relieved. The movie lot is overwhelming and big and I could easily get lost.

Soon we are at a building and he takes me right to a door that says "Director." And gives it a light knock and pushes on it.

Hunter's dad is on the phone and gestures for me to come in.

Oscar gives me a smile and says in a low voice, "Go get 'em, Tiger."

Then it's me alone standing like a doof while Mr. West talks about lights and contracts and other stuff that makes zero sense to me.

Finally, he hangs up, stands up and walks right past me and out the door.

I run to catch up with him. He talks over his shoulder to me.

"I'm going to pair you with Liza. She's one of the P.A.'s," he says. *Production Assistant.* "She'll show you the ropes the first day. We're starting on location in Hollywood."

I follow him mutely. I thought we *were* in Hollywood.

"What do you drive?" he asks suddenly, coming to a stop and facing me, his gaze intense.

"Um, a minivan," I say and cringe.

"Bingo!" His face lights up in a big smile. The first one I've ever seen on him. "You're going to drive the other P.A.'s and possibly extra crew to the location."

"Okay."

"On your way, stop and pick up a large vanilla cloud iced mocha with a sprinkle of cinnamon and cardamom."

"Okay."

I stand there staring at him.

"Well?" he says. "What are you waiting for? I'll send Liza to the crew parking lot with some of the other P.A.'s."

I freeze. But he's gone. So, I turn around and head back to the crew parking lot.

On the way there, I'm not really paying attention to the people passing me until I make eye contact with a beautiful boy and gasp as I recognize him. He's the star of one of my all-time favorite movies, *After*. When he realizes I've recognized him he gives me a sexy wink.

I rush past him before I can embarrass myself anymore. I grab my phone and text the girls. "First day on set and freaking Hero Fiennes Tiffin just walked by AND WINKED AT ME."

Coral responds first. "No way bitch!!!!!"

Emma is next. "I hate you. He's mine."

Paige is last. "That's right. I heard that he's filming a new movie. I met him once. He's a nice guy. His girlfriend is really sweet."

Then we all respond at once:

"You met him?"

"You've been holding out on us!"

"How could you not tell us this life-changing event?"

Then she sinks the knife in deeper. "I'm friends with him on Snapchat."

We all exclaim again and then I'm at my van.

I stand by it as more cars arrive and park and more people head toward the buildings. Several people stop at the food truck and walk away with breakfast burritos and green smoothies. And then a redheaded woman rushes over to me.

"You Kennedy?" she says. Her smile is quick but seems genuine. She has on skinny black pants and a silky green blouse with ballet flats. Her hair is pulled back in a messy bun and she has thick black plastic glasses. I'm suddenly grateful for Oscar's advice. I do fit in.

"Yes."

She thrusts out her hand. "I'm Liza. Let's get out of here."

"I thought a bunch of people were coming?" I say, lamely.

"Yeah. Change of plans. One carload already left. You and me will swing by and get the princess' latte."

"I was wondering about that," I say as Liza hops in the passenger seat of my van.

She hands me a card. "This will get you in out of the gate."

"Where in the hell am I supposed to get a latte with cardamom and who is it for, anyway?" I say.

Liza rolls her eyes. "Where? No clue. Who? The talent."

I grab my phone and speak into it: "Closest coffee shop with cardamom."

No surprise that my phone can't figure that puzzle out. We pull out of the lot right when Liza looks up from her phone and yells, "Turn right!"

I yank the steering wheel and we skid, but make the turn. My heart is pounding. We both burst into laughter.

In between giving me directions, Liza gives me the "rules":

"Rule #1: Don't bitch about anything. Got it?"

"No bitching."

"Rule #2: Don't gossip."

"Check."

"Rule #3: When you make a mistake—and believe me, you will—try to make up for it, learn from it, move on and be positive. No matter what."

I cringe but nod. I don't want to make mistakes.

A few minutes later we are in front of a coffee shop. "Double park here and I'll run in," Liza says.

She comes out with a large iced coffee. "And also, whatever you do, don't get on the wrong side of the talent."

"Define talent," I say. "Obviously, the stars, but are you talking about others?"

She shakes her head. "Not really. I mean the talent is basically the actors and the director. I mean you don't want to get on the bad side of anyone if you can help it, but you want to make sure you aren't pissing off the stars."

She looks over and gives me a once over that makes me squirm.

"Like you? You're super pretty so the lead actress is going to hate your fucking guts."

"That's stupid," I say, frowning.

Liza reaches out and grabs my shoulder. "You better take this seriously. I'm not kidding. It's not stupid. It's reality. Actresses are the most insecure people in the planet. I had one actress in forties who hated me because the director told me he liked the color of my hair once. That woman made my life hell the entire movie."

I sigh loudly. "And here I thought I was leaving the high school drama and bullshit behind."

She draws back and raises an eyebrow. "Not even close."

Just then a song comes on the radio and Liza reaches over and turns it up. "I hope you don't mind," she says. "I love this song."

It's Sunset Patrol.

I know the lead singer, Dylan. I met him at a Hollywood night club. But I keep my mouth shut. I can't just say I know him. It's much more involved and complicated than that

He's looking right at me. "Do you have a boyfriend? I mean do all of you have boyfriends?"

I blush at his intensity. But I nod. "We do."

I can't believe that he actually looks disappointed. I smile and shrug. "I'm sure you have lots of girlfriends, anyway. Or at least lots of options to find them."

He shakes his head and without looking at me brings his glass up to his lips and drains it.

"You'd be surprised."

I turn to Dylan and say in a low voice, "I find that hard to believe."

He exhales loudly. "It's hard to meet people."

I smirk.

He sees my face and holds up his palms. "I know, I know. It's totally

gross to hear me complain about anything. Poor Dylan. Has to tour the world and fight off screaming fans and can't find a real girl to hang out with."

My smirk vanishes looking into his eyes.

"It's not gross," I say, softly. "It probably is lonely."

He nods. "I don't really meet girls like you very much."

"What are girls like me?" I'm genuinely curious.

"Like I said, real girls. The girls I meet want to meet me because of who I am or because I have money or because maybe I can help their music career, or give them clout or ... yada, yada, yada, blah, blah, blah."

I take a sip of my glass. "That sucks."

While my friends are having a blast laughing and filming everyone on their phones, I sit here having a fairly intense and deep conversation with this famous guy. So, weird.

"How serious are you and your boyfriend?"

I frown. "Pretty serious."

"Oh."

I reach over and put my hand on his. "Listen, Dylan, I just met you but I have really good instincts on people and you seem like a really decent guy that any girl would be lucky to date."

He smiles and lifts my hand up and kisses my palm.

"Thank you for that, Kennedy Conner."

I tried to be friends with Dylan, but I realized I was playing with fire.

He has feelings for me and I just can't go there. My heart belongs to Hunter. Even when we were broken up and Dylan kissed me, he still wasn't Hunter.

Hunter is the boy I love.

Texting Dylan back or responding to his Snaps, even as friends, was leading him on. So, the last time he Snapped me, I left it undelivered. And he's not pursued it further.

I must have been quiet for a while because Liza looks over, "You like them?"

I smile. "Yeah," I say softly. "They're really good."

"And Dylan is smoking hot."

I smile again and nod. She's right. But he's so much more than that. He's funny and sweet and generous and has a big family he loves and if it wasn't for Hunter...in another life maybe.

Before she can talk more about him, we pull down the driveway of a beautiful house with a massive front lawn. There are several vans and people milling around the grounds lugging equipment into the back.

"The first scene is in the backyard," Liza says. "Park here."

I pull over and after we get out, she thrusts the iced coffee at me.

"I gotta go oversee the installation of fans and misters," she says looking up at the sky. "It's gonna be a hot one."

"Who am I supposed to..." I start to say.

She interrupts me and juts her chin toward a woman getting out of a black livery car. The woman has blonde hair trailing down her back and wears dark sunglasses under a thick fringe of blonde bangs. She has on a velvet track suit with high heels and steps out of the car as if there is an army of paparazzi about to snap her photo. I recognize her immediately.

She pauses, as if waiting for someone else to get out and sure enough the car door is still wide open.

Natalie.

4

The first thing I think is, *Hunter never told me that Natalie was the star of this movie!* All the times we talked about working on this film this summer her name never came up once.

I know I don't have a right to be, but I'm jealous and angry.

Hunter and Natalie are "friends." And I don't like it. They met in detox in Palm Springs and then both started attending the same daily AA meetings in Hollywood. It's one of the few meetings in the area that is just for teenagers.

For Hunter, it's a lifeline. His mother is a recovering addict and alcoholic and he's had some issues himself. He says that the meetings have made his life a million times better. So much so that he wants to someday become a sponsor for another teen.

I think it's a great idea. Younger teens who see how amazing Hunter is and then realize he doesn't drink? So many kids at our school look up to him. He's gorgeous, charismatic, and a super talented film maker. Not to mention a great basketball player.

The only part I don't like is how much time he spends with the other people in his AA group. I know it's petty, but they share something with him that I don't.

And that means gorgeous It Girl actress Natalie shares something with him I don't. But I trust him. I really do. I'm just not sure how much I trust her.

Hunter claims she's madly in love with her rock star boyfriend, but she's a bit of a diva so I think she'd love to have my boyfriend wrapped around her little finger, too, as a consolation prize.

A while back Hunter and I were having some problems—really a misunderstanding—and Natalie pounced on it. Her boyfriend was out of the country during some big club opening so she asked Hunter to fill in and go with her.

The paparazzi spotted them together and went wild. By dawn the next day, photos of Natalie and Hunter were everywhere along with articles questioning who Natalie's new mystery man was.

I've just pulled the minivan into the parking lot at school when my phone explodes. I put the van in park and start pulling up texts and messages and snaps.

The first one is a text from a number I don't recognize. I open it and stare in shock at the picture that loads.

It's Hunter. With a blonde girl. They are holding hands and seem to be running away from a crowd of photographers with flashbulbs going off. The picture is from some tabloid. It has a caption, "Natalie Austin spotted at Hollywood Nightclub with sexy mystery man. Sources say he left longtime girlfriend to be with starlet."

Suddenly I can't breathe. I'm doubled over in pain, pressing my fore-head on the steering wheel. My face feels icy cold. There is not enough air in the car. I want to throw open my door and run, screaming at the same time I want to curl up in the fetal position in my van. But I'm too paralyzed to do anything but stare at the van's dashboard.

Finally, when I catch my breath, I sit back up and start to read the messages and texts.

Coral: "What the fuck?"

Paige: "I swear I didn't know."

Emma: "I'm sorry. Where are you?"

Nothing from Hunter. Nothing.

I'm shaking as I open and read message after message.

A few Snap DM's from people I barely know. A few girls say random things, such as "You're way prettier than her" and "He's a jerk. You're better off without him."

Then the guys apparently feel the need to weigh in. I read them all, still feeling as if I'm in shock. Nothing seems real. A cute boy from my math class Snaps a DM: "He's a fool."

Another guy writes, "Oof. You're cute. Want to hang out." I don't even remember who he is and his bitmoji doesn't help me remember.

Then of course there are a few anonymous nasty ones.

One person writes that Hunter was smart to finally ditch my ugly ass and get with a girl who deserves him.

As soon as I read it, I know who wrote the next one: "I told you, New Girl. Hunter only likes the bright new shiny things. You're old news, bitch. Welcome to the club of those who have fucked Hunter West and then are left in the dust."

Ava. Fucking bitch.

Shortly after that, Hunter and I made up and he promises me that Natalie's not a threat. I believe him. But now I wonder why the hell he never mentioned she was the star of the movie we were both working on all summer?

As soon as I think this, Hunter emerges from the same black car.

A bitter taste fills my mouth. My stomach roils with jealousy. Especially when I see the smile she gives him as he emerges. She waits for him to fall into step and they both disappear into the house.

I can feel the scowl on my face. I don't trust her as far as I can throw her.

I swallow the acid taste in my mouth and start after them with the latte. The entire plastic cup is sweating with condensation and its wet and slippery. I hurry to catch up. They are at the top of the stairs to the house when I reach the bottom step and damn if I'm going to yell after her to stop or wait, so I race up the stairs.

Hunter must sense something or hear me behind him because he turns at the exact moment I trip at the top step and the drink goes flying out of my hand and explodes onto Natalie right when she turns to see what Hunter is looking at. Her blood curdling scream and string of expletives is the backdrop to the horror I feel.

Her pale pink velvet tracksuit is now coated with latte. With Cardamom.

She is beet red and flinging her hands around and sputtering obscenities.

Hunter is instantly at my side—where I am on the ground at the top step. "Kennedy, are you okay?"

My Michael Kors black pants that fit like a dream now have a hole in the knee. My palms are skinned and bleeding. Hunter is crouched on the step beside where I'm sitting. He brushes off my palms. I have tears in my eyes.

I've already fucked up.

Natalie's incessant bitching above us makes it clear that there can't possibly be one person within a five-mile radius that isn't aware of her outrage. Everyone is staring. I feel like a fool.

Hunter lifts my chin and when he meets my eyes I blink to fight back tears.

"I'm sorry," I say. What I want to say is, "Why the hell didn't you tell me she was starring in this movie?"

"You don't have to apologize," Hunter says, and now I want to cry even more. "You tripped. I'm more worried about whether you're okay."

He leans over and gives me a hug.

When he does the screeching behind us goes dead silent.

Natalie must have realized that Hunter is completely ignoring her and attending to me. I look up. Her mouth is clamped shut. Her eyes narrow and I know I've already broken one of Liza's cardinal rules — do not make enemies with the talent.

Too late.

LIZA SAVES THE DAY.

Before Hunter helps me to my feet, Liza is there.

She is dabbing at Natalie's tracksuit.

"Good thing you haven't changed into wardrobe yet," Liza says.

Natalie's eyes are pure steel and she is not taking them off me.

"Hunter," she says, still looking at me. "Can you come with me to wardrobe so I can figure out what to wear?"

I stare at her, my mouth wide open. Who the fuck does she think she is? Is Hunter her errand boy? And what is she implying? That he be in her dressing room as she changes?

He answers distractedly. "Um, I'm going to take Kennedy to the first aid station and get her palms looked at."

Wrong answer.

She tosses her hair back and then sees something past us. I turn to look.

It's Hunter's dad.

"What's going on?" he says loping up the stairs.

Natalie gives him a tight smile. "Your new P.A. tripped and spilled my latte."

I can see his face blanch. And I want to die.

"I'm so sorry," I say, again, this time looking at Natalie.

She gives me a queenly nod.

"It's fine," she says. "I don't care about this old tracksuit anyway. I have a million of them, but I really did need that latte. Do you think you could be a dear and go fetch me another one?"

She said fetch. *Fetch.* I realize my mouth is wide open. I shut it quickly. I am brushing my pants off. "Of course." I reach for my phone. "I'll find a place close by and be back in a few minutes."

"What about your hands?" Hunter says.

I smile at him. "I'll be fine."

I turn to leave but freeze when Natalie speaks again.

"Actually," she says. "Not to be a bother, but I really do need the exact same drink." She squints her eyes and peers down at the plastic cup on the ground. "One from Westwood Beanery."

Hunter makes a noise and his dad's head swivels toward him.

Hunter clears his throat and says, "The beanery is forty minutes away, with traffic, it's going to take nearly three hours for her to get there and get back."

"Just go," Mr. West says to me. And then he turns to Hunter. "It's her first day. She's learning the ropes. It's not always glamorous being a P.A. She might as well learn that right off the bat."

Hunter opens his mouth as if to protest but then closes it. He closes his eyes and then opens them to give me a sympathetic look. I know he's not going to stand up to his dad. And neither am I.

"Of course," I say.

The smug smile on Natalie's face makes my blood boil.

I couldn't be happier when Hunter leans over and kisses me goodbye on the mouth and when he draws back I see that her smile has disappeared.

But I know better than to be too happy.

I've made a serious enemy.

5

What a waste of time.

I didn't get home from my first day until seven and fell into bed exhausted, thinking about my day and how it had all gone terribly wrong.

Along with tripping and spilling the drink on the star of the movie, effectively humiliating myself in front of, well—everyone—I also made an enemy of said star. And she made it clear I knew this.

I spent 90-minutes making the trip back to the stupid coffee shop to get her a replacement latte.

When I got back, hot and sweaty (the minivan's air conditioning decided today was a good day to quit) I managed to find Natalie in a spare bedroom getting her makeup done between shoots. I came in and there was a rolling rack of costume changes and she sat before a vanity with one woman fixing her hair and another doing her makeup.

I put the latte on the vanity without speaking and turned to go.

But as I did, I saw her reach for it and take a sip. I kept walking.

I heard her say, "Excuse me," so I stopped. But she wasn't talking to me. She was telling the woman doing her makeup. But still I watched in the mirror as she lifted the lid off the drink and poured it into a trash can, keeping her eyes on me the entire time.

Then she smiled and shrugged. "I just don't feel like drinking it anymore."

When I finally found Liza, she put me to work loading and unloading props from different trucks. Once I was done with that, and even more sweaty, I helped Liza set up giant fans that would be out of sight but keep the actors cool during scenes in the backyard.

At one point, I got to stand and watch a scene. And it gave me a glimpse of Hunter. He was shadowing the sound guy with the big boom mics. When he walked onto the set he smiled and winked and my whole shitty morning disappeared.

Then Natalie came out to the pool in a skimpy bikini and I suddenly felt like I looked like a boy compared to her curves.

When she first walked out of the house, she paused. I could see her eyes seek out Hunter and I wanted to kill her. He was busy talking but I could tell when he saw her. He looked over at her and I could see him stop speaking when he saw her. But then he quickly looked away.

I'd never been so jealous in my life. But still happy he looked away.

I hated to admit it, but when Natalie performed her scene, I was mesmerized. She really was a good actress. Instead of Natalie, she became Dusty, the teenage daughter of an organized crime figure. Liza had explained the plot briefly during our drive in the morning. Dusty's father was going to get on the wrong side of some other crime figures and Dusty was going to be kidnapped.

But meanwhile, Dusty was falling hard for Dominic, her father's right hand man, a gorgeous guy in his twenties. When the actor playing Dominic first came on the set, Liza and I exchanged glances. She mouthed, "Whoa."

I nodded.

He was wearing a black silk shirt and black slacks with shiny shoes. His dark hair was swept back and he had piercing onyx eyes. He was the other big star of the film. I could see why.

And during the scene between Natalie and him, I could feel the sexual tension. He'd walked out to the pool to say something to her, but then stopped dead when he saw her in her bikini in the lounge chair. You could read his emotions. He wanted her. But she was the boss's daughter.

Then she turned over and asked him to put sunscreen on her back and he did. The cameras got in super close and I could see on the screen by us how they zoomed in on his hand rubbing the lotion on her skin and how she began to squirm. And then his hand dipped lower and snuck under the top of her barely there bikini bottoms. Just then, Dusty's dad yelled from inside the house and Dominic jumped back as if he were burned. He stood just as the dad came out.

Hunter's dad yelled "cut" and everyone started congratulating the two on the scene.

Natalie looked bored at the praise and, ignoring everyone, walked inside.

But the actor playing Dominic seemed to soak up the admiration.

I looked for Hunter and he was bent over some sound equipment in a seemingly intense discussion with the guy doing sound.

"Oh, my God," Liza said. "I've almost never seen one take on something before. That was a one-take scene, girlfriend. Don't expect that to happen very often."

"It was hot," I said.

"Damn straight."

And she was right, the next several scenes were performed over and over before the director and producer found them acceptable.

Toward the end of the day I happen to be getting a drink at the drinking fountain when the actor playing Dominic comes out of the bathroom.

"You were great today," I say.

He pauses. "Thanks." He stops walking and I freeze.

"What's your name?" He's got an English accent.

"What? You're English? Your American accent is brilliant."

"Thanks, love," he says. "But you never gave me your name."

"Kennedy."

He gives a slow smile.

"What you doing later, Kennedy? The director here has put me up in a really glam L.A. penthouse and I just got a delivery of some blow and could use the company tonight. You game?"

Instantly he's lost all his attractiveness to me. I smile and say, "Oh sorry. I have plans with my boyfriend."

He tilts his head to look at me. "Too bad, love."

I smile and rush away.

Fuck. What a player. And pervert. He's got to be nearly thirty if not over.

Now, lying in bed, I replay the day over in my mind and decide that I was wrong: it wasn't a bad first day after all. Despite a rough beginning, I actually had spent my first full day on a movie set and that in itself was exciting.

Just then my phone rings. I reach for it in the dark.

It's Hunter.

"How was your first day?" he asks.

"Crazy. You?"

"Same. I'm sorry about the morning thing. Natalie can be difficult sometimes."

"You think?"

Then I wait a few seconds before plunging right in. "Why didn't you tell me she was starring in this film." I purposely say "she" instead of her name.

"Didn't I? I thought I did."

"No."

"Oh. I guess I thought you knew."

"Nope."

"Sorry."

And with that one word, all my irritation at him not telling me disappears. We've been through a lot this past year, I'm not going to let my jealousy cause a problem.

"It's okay."

"I miss you," he says.

"Me, too. How was your meeting?"

He and Natalie left set early to attend their AA meeting. It was hard to watch them walk off set together. But at the same time, I know how important those meetings are to Hunter so I was grateful his dad was making accommodations for him to attend.

His dad actually stops filming and the crew takes a break while Natalie and Hunter attend the meeting. When they get back, the filming starts back up again. Because of this, though, our day might sometimes go as late as nine or ten, Liza had said. She said the P.A.'s were often excused early, though. Like I was tonight.

"The meeting was cool," Hunter says. "They all wanted to meet up after I got off work, but I'm beat. I'm home."

He yawns and as he does, says, "Got a five-a.m. call."

"Go to sleep."

"Okay," He mumbles. "Night."

"Night."

I hang up, set my phone down on the nightstand, close my eyes, and that is that.

6

I wake in the dark and quickly shower and dress.

Luckily, Oscar had convinced me to buy several variations of the black pants, black shirt outfit so I have another pair of pants that aren't ripped to wear today.

Oscar has already left. His call was even earlier than mine.

I manage to find the movie lot on my own this time, and when I show the guard my card he opens the gate. That's kind of cool.

I park in the crew parking lot and order a green smoothie from the food truck. I chat with a few people my age in the food line and then Liza appears.

"Chop, chop, pumpkin," she says "Today, we're building a set in the A building."

The set stuff takes up most of the day. I don't see Hunter or Natalie at all. Liza says that everyone else is in a different building shooting a scene in Dusty's bedroom. I wonder, but don't ask if it's a sex scene. And then I wonder if Hunter is going to be there watching it? Ugh.

I remind myself that I'm not the jealous type, but I'm not sure I'm convincing enough.

I leave for the day at seven without having seen Hunter once. I'm disappointed. But I'm not here to catch glimpses or exchange glances with my boyfriend, I'm here to learn about being on a film set.

Days blend into one another. Sometimes Hunter and I are working close by and we can smile and even once we took a quick break together. But for the most part, Liza has me running around doing errands. I guess it's all typical P.A. stuff from what I've heard. There are about six of us who are basically grunts. So much for me working for Mr. Hunter directly. I don't know if I misunderstood or he changed his mind, but I rarely see him and if we cross paths he doesn't even say hello. But then again, he doesn't give anyone on set the time of day. He's always so intense and busy.

Somehow Dominic manages to find me and leer at me at least once a day, but I'm always cheery and fake and able to slip away pretty easily.

"He's got the hots for you," Liza says. "I'd watch out. He's probably got more STD's than Warren Beatty and they say he slept with 12,000 women."

"Who?" I ask

"Never mind," she says.

Finally, it's Friday. Hunter and I have plans to get together when he gets home. I know it could be late. Luckily me and the other P.A.s aren't on his intense schedule.

I'm so tired, but also excited to see him, so I'm dressed with my makeup fixed at ten waiting for him to either call or show up.

Instead he texts me.

"Hellish day. I'm still on set."

"Really?"

"Long story."

"Oh."

"I'm sorry. Can I come over in a.m.?"

"Sure," I say, trying to hide my disappointment.

The next day Hunter knocks on our door at nine. He is so damn cute that I fall into his arms. I can't stop smiling. He hugs me so tight.

"Oh God, I missed you," he says. "It's torture to have you that close without being able to talk to you or touch you."

"Totally," I say.

"What do you want to do?"

I grab his hand and lead him inside with a smile.

"Wait? What about your mom?"

I tell him that my mom and Oscar went to Pasadena to the flea market.

He gets a wicked smile. "They'll be gone for hours."

"Exactly," I say.

Later, we go out to breakfast with the rest of our remaining friend group: Paige and Coral and Dex and Devin. We send Emma a selfie of us making sad faces. I miss that girl.

Over breakfast burritos we all decide to spend the day at the beach. I can't wait. It's how I imagined my summer would be.

The rest of the weekend is every summer movie I ever wanted to live in my own life. We stay at the beach until late Saturday night and then meet again around ten the next day to do it all over again. We drink sodas spiked with booze and eat snacks and play volleyball and splash in the waves and nap and read in the sun.

It's a dream come true for this Brooklyn girl who grew up watching movies about California kids who lived by the beach.

But soon it's Sunday night.

Hunter drops me off at my house. My skin is still warm from the sun and I have sand still lightly sticking to my arms and bare feet. I learned early on that it's nearly impossible to live by the beach and avoid having sand everywhere. But I wouldn't trade it for anything.

I tell Hunter not to bother walking me to the door, he needs to get home to bed. His call is at five a.m. I lean in his open window to kiss him goodbye.

"Thanks for the great weekend," he says.

It was great. We even managed to squeeze in a few sessions of sex at his room over the garage. All in all, a perfect weekend.

"You too," I say and then as I walk away, I say dryly, "See you next weekend."

He makes a face. "I wish that wasn't true but it might be."

We lock eyes and then he starts his car. I stand in the doorway and watch his Jeep until it pulls out of the driveway.

7

On Wednesday, we have a huge key scene to film. But everybody is out of sorts and off their cues. Hunter's dad and the producer argue all morning about the film footage they are periodically reviewing. Natalie flounces off set more than once and different P.A.s have to go talk her into coming back.

Liza looks at me the third time it happens. "Don't worry. You won't have to deal with her."

"Oh." I wonder if Liza is worried about me upsetting Natalie more since she might associate me with the spilled latte.

"Remember when I told you not to make enemies of the talent?" Liza asks.

"How could I forget?"

"Well, after the Latte Incident on Day 1, Natalie made it clear you're not to go near her. At first I thought this was your death knell, but for some reason Mr. West is keeping you onboard. But be careful. Princess doesn't like you and doesn't like that the director took your side over hers. I've heard rumors."

My side over Natalie's? I find that hard to believe. I open my mouth to say a whole hell of a lot of things I should keep to myself.

Liza looks over at me and I press my lips tightly together. One of the rules was not to gossip. So at least I can try to follow that rule.

Because what I want to say is that the main reason Natalie doesn't like me because I'm Hunter's girlfriend. But I don't know if anyone else on set knows this. I haven't told Liza.

And besides, it doesn't necessarily mean that Natalie likes Hunter, either. He claims she's crazy about her rock star boyfriend. But I have my doubts. What's clear is that she doesn't like sharing the spotlight with anyone. For any reason. Ever.

The afternoon drags on and still the shot the producer and director are looking for isn't happening. Natalie and the actor playing Dominic are on their tenth or so take. I have to admit that I'm impressed by how professional they seem. They aren't arguing or complaining. They just do the take over and over.

But I think this too soon because right after, Natalie throws a hissy fit worthy of Marie Antoinette. She throws things. She screams. She actually rips off the sweater she's supposed to wear in the scene and stomps off telling Hunter's dad and the producer to "fuck off."

Me and the other P.A.'s look at each other with our mouths wide open.

Mr. West goes over to where Hunter is set up and speaks to him for a few seconds. I see Hunter nod and then he walks in the same direction where Natalie went.

I don't like it one bit.

A few minutes later, Mr. West announces that filming is going to resume again at six. I know this is usually when Natalie and Hunter return from their AA meeting.

But the meeting doesn't start until four. And it's only two.

Liza walks over to speak to Mr. Hunter and then returns, gathering me and all the other P.A.s around her.

"It's your lucky day," she says. "You're off until tomorrow. Don't go nuts. See you in the morning—bright and early."

I'm home by three and hardly know what to do with myself.

I change out of my work clothes and into some cut off jean shorts and a super soft T-shirt.

Then I fix a smoothie and text Paige and Coral.

"Hey, bitches. Off early. Want to do something?"

Instead of a text, Coral calls me.

When I answer, I can tell she's crying.

"What's wrong?" I say, alarm zinging through me.

"It's Dex. Even though they say he's back to normal, there's some things..." she trails off.

"What do you mean, Coral?" I ask. "What things? He seemed normal last weekend."

Josh Masters and friends beat Dex so bad he landed in the hospital with a brain injury. He's better now. Or at least we thought so.

I called Dex," Coral says. "No answer. I texted. Same. So, I called and texted Devin and he didn't answer, either. I drove straight to their houses and their SUV was gone."

As Coral speaks, I'm reaching into my closet to pull on a sweatshirt and leggings, shedding my flannel pajama pants as I do.

"Then—"

"You went to Hunters," I interrupt. "And they weren't there, either?"

Hunter's Jeep was gone.

"Fuck."

"Where do you think they are?" she asks.

I pause. "The beach or the basketball court."

"I'm at the beach," she says. "I'll meet you at the basketball court."

I'm already out the door and starting my minivan.

I didn't leave a note for Mom or Oscar but they can text me if they're worried.

Right now, I'm too freaked out.

I'm afraid of what will happen when Josh and his friends meet up with Hunter and his. It's going to be bad. Really bad. I wonder if I should call 911.

Coral calls and we talk the entire drive.

"I'm sick to my stomach," she says.

"Me, too."

"I'm almost there."

"Me, too."

As soon as I pull into the parking lot I see two dozen cars or so at the far end near the basketball courts and baseball fields. It's pretty dark but I with the streetlights I can see a bunch of people gathered in the middle of the baseball field.

Coral's car pulls in right behind me. I pull partway onto the field and jump out, heading toward the dugout. I can hear shouting and screams now.

I push my way through the crowd with both hands, physically shoving people out of my way to clear a path. Coral is on my heels. When we get close to the center, all I see is a mass of bodies wrestling and throwing punches. Two guys are on the ground, grappling and throwing punches. I'm searching for Hunter. Of course, he's squared off with Josh. They are leaning into one another throwing punches like it's a boxing match. They then part and back off and go for it again. Hunter manages to loop an arm around Josh's neck and is punching him in the face when I hear Coral let loose with a blood curdling scream right beside me.

Everything stops and it grows quiet as she races over to a figure on the ground. Someone is standing over the guy kicking him in the face.

The guy freezes, boot in mid-kick. Coral is kneeling down now. It's Dex.

She's wailing and crying and cradling his head. Then she looks up wild-eyed and screams. "Call 911! Call 911!"

People start to run away. I look around wild-eyed and reach for my phone. I punch in the numbers and shakily tell the dispatcher we need an ambulance. Someone is badly hurt.

I give her our address and then say, "Hurry! Now! Hurry! Please!"

She assures me someone is coming and asks for my number to call back.

I give it to her. Devin is on his knees now beside Dex. Hunter is standing there above them with his head in his hands.

I rush over to Coral. "They're coming."

I'm afraid to look down at Dex. His eyes are not open. He looks dead.

"I didn't want to say anything at first because I wasn't sure it meant anything, but he gets confused," Coral says. "Like he thought that we had graduated last night."

"Oh, no," I say. Graduation was two weeks ago. I feel sick hearing this.

"Today, when we were going to Laguna, he went down wrong way roads not once but twice."

"Oh shit."

"I know."

"What does he say about it?" I ask.

"He just says his brain is still goofy."

"Is this normal? Did he say what the doctor told him about stuff like this?"

"That's the thing," she says. "His doctor visits are over. I mean, he could go see a doctor, but his last follow-up appointment with the neurologist was a few weeks ago."

I think about it for a few seconds. "I think you just need to say something. I know it will suck, but you need to say that you're concerned because of these things he's done. And you can ask him if the doctor told him this was normal. Because, Coral, it might be. I mean, I don't know about this stuff, but I've heard it can take a year to recover from a concussion and what happened to him was worse than that."

She's quiet. For a long time.

"Coral?"

She's weeping. "I want to fucking kill Josh Masters. Murder him. Dead."

I sigh loudly. "Me, too."

"Let's take him out," she says.

"I wish."

"No, really."

I don't answer.

"He needs to pay for what he's done: to you, to Hunter, to Dex."

I don't answer.

"I've tried to take the higher ground," she says. "Forgive your enemy and all that shit that my parents and my church teach me. But I'm sick of being nice. Fuck nice. Nice people get shit on. I want to be a bad ass, a bad girl like those bitches Ava and Carly. A girl that nobody fucks with."

Again, I don't answer.

"You don't want to be the bad girl?" Coral asks.

"I didn't say that."

I END up staying home and watching a bunch of 1980s teen flicks—The Breakfast Club and Fast Times at Ridgemont High and Pretty in Pink—and then crawling into bed early.

Hunter texts me that he misses me. But when I write back, he doesn't reply again.

As I get ready for bed, I think about Coral's call.

The thought that Dex could have permanent brain damage because of Josh Masters makes me sick to my stomach. It also makes me furious.

And I realize that yes, I do want Josh Masters to pay. Not with his life like she said jokingly. But I do want him to pay.

But I have no idea how to make this happen. When I turned to the justice system, it let me down. It let a lying conniving bitch like Ava to submit fake evidence and derail the whole thing. How can I trust it again?

I can't.

If anyone is a "bad girl" as Coral put it, it's Ava.

That woman has made my life hell from my first class on my first day at Pacific High.

I guess she and Hunter had a brief thing years ago and he spurned her and she's never forgiven him. On the first day of class with the three of us, he made it clear that he wanted to make me his, and she instantly disliked me.

Over the weeks and months, she was usually just rude, but it got increasingly worse.

The final blow was after Josh Masters assaulted me and Ava tried to make it look like it was consensual. She fabricated a story and manipulated a video tape in his defense.

I'll never forget that day in court with Ava dressed all in white and me all in black and the judge calling the attorneys into his chambers.

Ultimately, the judge decided not hold Josh over for trial.

Why would one girl do that to another girl? I could understand her not liking me, but to stoop that low? It just didn't make sense.

Josh Masters walked away free with zero consequences for attempting to rape me.

There has to be some way to make sure Josh doesn't ever hurt anybody again.

I fall asleep tossing and turning and wishing I knew just how to do that.

few days later, the answer comes to me in the most unexpected way. A way I never thought would happen in my wildest imagination.

Ava—of all people—comes to me for help.

My phone dings and I look down.

I don't recognize the number but I open the message.

"It's Ava. Can we talk?"

I frown. There's no way this can be anything but trouble.

"Why?"

"I want to tell you in person."

"This sounds like a set up," I write.

"I promise it's not."

"Your word means nothing to me."

"I deserve that." She writes.

My inclination is to ignore her and I'm about to set my phone down when she writes something else: "It's about Josh. I need your help."

I still don't trust her. It could be a trap. But I can't help but wonder and I know I will meet her. But not during my precious weekend when I can spend time with Hunter. I know he has plans with his mother Monday after work and his dad has agreed to let him go even if they aren't done filming.

Hunter's mom had a relapse on her sobriety but has been clean and sober for a few weeks. She is supposed to be checking out of the Palm Springs detox center tomorrow and Hunter is going to meet her at her new apartment in Venice after work on Monday. Hunter's dad rented a small studio apartment for her that used to be a garage space. Hunter says it's nice, though. Despite Mr. West's brusque demeanor, I must say he always takes care of his ex-wife.

I wonder what his new wife—Paige's mother—thinks. I don't know her very well. She's a corporate lawyer and seems to be overseas traveling half the time. I have a feeling she probably encourages Mr. West to help his ex.

Although he's intimidating, Hunter's dad also is understanding of teenage stuff. For instance, Natalie is a teenager and so are a lot of the P.A.s, so he said we get weekends off.

Liza told me that this isn't always the case.

My curiosity is greater than my lingering anger at Ava so I agree. So, sure I'll meet with her. On my terms.

"Monday 8 p.m. Balboa Beach parking lot," I text her.

"Thanks."

Just her typing "thanks" has me even more suspicious.

9

I spend the weekend with Hunter at the beach.

Everybody else is busy so we spend both days alone. Which is fine by me. I love our friend group, but since I barely ever see Hunter during the week, I don't mind spending some time alone with him.

We read and snack and work on our tans and splash in the water and take long walks. Then Saturday night we pick up a pizza at our favorite place and head home. We take the pizza down to Oscar's basement theater room and watch movies.

Oscar and my mom go to bed early so after the movies, we sneak out on the back deck and have sex on the massive lounge chair.

"How am I going to go six months without this," I say when we are done.

"Tell me about it," he says.

"In all seriousness, though," I say leaning my head on his shoulder. "I'm going to miss every second with you. This. But also, just sitting around watching movies and laughing."

"Same, Boots. Same."

Hunter is the perfect boyfriend for me. We are both super

passionate about movies and becoming filmmakers. Sometimes I wonder how I got so lucky.

But then I remember darkly that my life wasn't always like this. A year ago, I was depressed and anxious and worried that my dad was going to end up killing my mom in an alcoholic rage.

On some days, it feels like a distant memory, something I read in a book or that happened to someone else.

Sunday morning, Coral calls me. She talked to Dex about his confusion. He's agreed to make another appointment and get checked out.

I'm glad but hearing this makes me angrier than ever at Josh. He's hurt so many people and walked away without a single consequence. It's not fair.

I can't wait to hear what Ava says. I worry it's a trap, but my desire for revenge is stronger. I'll take the risk.

I'm on set Monday night until 7 p.m. By the time I get home, I'm regretting making plans to meet Ava. And I feel guilty not telling Hunter about it.

He had texted me after I got home, saying he just got back from meeting his mom and would probably have to work until ten. He also asked what I was doing.

I wrote back that I missed him, but didn't answer his question about what I was up to.

I arrive at the Balboa Beach parking lot early and sit in my car listening to music.

For a second I wonder if I should've told someone I was meeting her. Since she lied in court, she's capable of just about anything, I figure.

A brand new pale pink VW bug pulls up beside me. I can tell by the flash of brilliant white blonde hair under the streetlight that it's Ava. I get out and walk over to her car.

"Want to get in?" she says. "It's kind of cold."

I hesitate. She swallows and looks down. "I swear, Kennedy, I'm on the up and up here. I need your help."

She looks up at me now and I see tears in her eyes. Either she's as good an actor as Natalie, or she means it.

I walk over to the passenger door and climb inside. It smells like cotton candy inside her car and she has a fancy coffee drink in the console. She takes a sip.

When she sets it back down, she says, "Sorry. I didn't ask if you wanted something. I'm just nervous and need the caffeine boost to help me say what I need to say."

"I'm good," I say, and relax into the seat.

She doesn't start the engine just stares out at the black sea before us. It's cold and cloudy tonight so the beach and its parking lot are deserted. A chill races down my back and I don't know if it's apprehension or the cold.

"I met Josh the summer before he started going to school at Pacific High," Ava says, still staring out the front windshield. "We met at a party at Chad's house. I was drunk and we started kissing and then he led me into a bedroom upstairs. I realized now he must have given me something, some date rape drug, because I don't remember anything after I got to the bedroom and started kissing him."

She gives a long shuddering sigh.

I want to reach out to her and touch her shoulder but my hand stops in mid-air. This is Ava. The girl who made my life hell.

My hands are suddenly clenched in fists. I can see Josh inches in front of me backing me up to the crashing waves. If Hunter hadn't have come along Josh would've raped me right then and there.

Ava continues.

"When school started, I found out that people had been talking about me—spreading rumors about me being with the football team that night, but I didn't remember anything," she says. "Josh said to ignore them. That I was super drunk and just passed out. And that was it."

I remember the rumor I'd heard about her my first week at school and how I had used that against her once. I suddenly feel more shame than I can handle. I swallow a bitter taste in my mouth and wish I could take it all back. Even though she's done some horrible things to me. I still would take it back if I could.

Ava puts her forehead down on the steering wheel now.

"I believed him."

Until last weekend.

His parents were out of town and he got really drunk.

Ava was drinking too. She told him that she loved him but that she felt really bad about lying to the judge. She said she wanted me to pay for falsely accusing him, but that she was worried the judge would realize the video was doctored.

"I told him I had nightmares about getting caught," she says.

Josh freaked out.

He said she was stupid to think he loved her. That he didn't even like her. She was just an easy fuck for him. He said every night he wasn't with her, he was fucking other girls and even going to prostitutes to give him what she wouldn't.

"And then he told me that I *did* have sex with the football team. And that it was not only on videotape but that Chad's dad had walked in and saw the whole thing and didn't care," she says and starts to cry.

"What did you say?" I ask.

She slapped him and tried to leave the house, but he stopped her. And beat her.

As she says this, she lifts her shirt up.

"He's good at hitting you where it doesn't show," she says. Her back and side are covered in bruises.

"Oh, my God," I say. I feel like I'm going to vomit.

"I'm afraid to go to the police. He's gotten away with this for a long time with lots of girls. I can't take the chance that for some reason I'll be the one the police believe. Not with my record. At least not by myself."

"You have a record?"

She nods and closes her eyes. "A drug arrest. He'll make sure it's brought up and say I was high on drugs and that someone else beat me. That's what he threatened to do if I didn't fix the videotape of you that night. He'll send it to the admissions people at Loyola Marymount."

"That's awful but it wouldn't matter, would it? I mean they wouldn't kick you out, would they?" I ask.

"I don't know. It's a Catholic school. I don't know anything," she says. "Except if I don't get in there, my life is over. My parents will disown me. I have a full scholarship there now. It's my only chance to go to college."

Finally, she lifts her head and looks at me. "Do you think this is all bullshit?"

"I believe you," I say.

Coral had dug up some dirt that showed the reason he left his old school in Reno and came to Pacific High was because he'd tried to rape a girl in his old town. For some reason those charges, like mine, had been dropped.

I sit there silently as she pulls down her visor mirror and wipes away streaks of black eye makeup. When she's done, she turns to me again.

I'm quiet for a few moments and then I say what I've been thinking.

"I'm still mad at you. I know that he pressured you into what you did, but you were never nice to me from day one. And yeah, I get that you were miserable and taking it out on everyone else, but I think you owe me an apology. With that said, I am truly sorry that all that happened to you. Nobody deserves that. Josh is a monster. And he's only going to get worse. But what I can't figure out is why you care coming to me and telling me all of this," I say. "Are you looking for my forgiveness?"

She inhales and then exhales loudly. "I'm asking you to help me make Josh Masters pay for what he did to us so he never does it to another girl again."

We lock eyes. After a few seconds, I nod. "I'm in."

10

On Tuesday, Hunter's dad tells everyone it's going to be a late night. There were some "hiccups" last week with filming and we are behind schedule.

"Plan on staying until at least ten tonight," he says.

Liza rolls her eyes. "So much for my date. Welcome to the glamorous life on a movie set."

Around 3:30, Hunter's dad calls a break. I see Hunter and Natalie leave. It's become normal now, everyone heads to the food truck for an early dinner and then filming resumes around six when the star returns.

Liza says this is crazy. "I've never personally seen a director accommodate an actress this way, but I know it happens. The bigger the star, the bigger diva they are. This one is just getting started. Just wait."

I get street tacos at the food truck and eat them alone in my minivan with the air conditioning on and my L.A. summer playlist on. It has songs that remind me of hanging at the beach with Hunter.

It has "Reflections" by The Neighborhood and "Dirty Iyanna" by Youngboy Never Broke Again and "Sunflower" by Post Malone and Swae Lee.

Our break is only until 4:30 and then Liza and I are back to work, getting the next scene ready for when Natalie returns. In this scene, she and Dominic are at a fancy restaurant.

Liza and I work on the set, but also rounding up the extras who will be other diners and the restaurant staff. Everyone gets assigned a seat and a spot.

We're so busy that I don't realize that six o'clock has come and gone until Liza frowns and looks at her watch. I take out my phone. It's 6:30.

Then at seven, Hunter's dad comes onto the set and starts screaming in a booming voice. "Where are my actors?"

Dominic and another main character step into the light.

"Where in the hell?"

And then to my shock, he stomps over to me. His face is bright red and he looks down at me.

"Where is Hunter?"

Everyone looks at me and exchanges glances. I haven't told a soul, not even Liza, that Hunter and I are dating. I shrug. "Last I saw or heard from him was when he left at 3:30."

I swallow.

"Text him," he demands. "He won't return my texts maybe he'll answer yours."

My face is growing hot so I know I'm blushing like mad. Liza has a "What the fuck?" look on her face.

"I'll explain later," I say to her under my breath as I dip my head to my phone and text Hunter:

"Your dad is freaking out and wants me to find where you are. Where are you, anyway?"

I send it and then stare at my phone screen for a few seconds. I don't see the telltale three dots telling me he is writing back. Nothing. Finally, I look up at Liza who has her hands on her hips.

"Fine," I say. "Hunter is my boyfriend."

"Jesus Christ. You think you might have said something sooner?"

"Sorry." Even I know I sound lame.

"No wonder Natalie hates you."

"What?" I say whirling, my face hot with anger.

"Well clearly you are the competition."

"Whatever."

Then she tilts her head. "Doesn't it drive you crazy they are always together? I thought they were dating since they always take off to meetings together."

"See why I didn't say anything?" I say.

"Yeah, but, Kennedy, how do you deal?"

I think about it for a second and then say. "He says they're just friends. And I believe him. I trust him."

Liza exhales loudly. "Well, bully for you."

I shrug. "Like I said, there's a reason I didn't say anything."

I walk off and not sure what to do with myself go to the bathroom. In my stall, I try not to cry. Where *is* Hunter?

11

I refuse to text him again.

I have my pride, after all.

Even though it's now mortally wounded on the movie set. Every person there now knows that we are dating and that he and Natalie have disappeared. Together.

But I refuse to feel humiliated.

I don't care what a bunch of strangers think of me.

But I do care what he thinks of me, despite it all, and I'm not going to be his doormat.

And part of me is worried sick.

There have been times in the past when he hasn't returned my calls or text and nine times out of ten it was because he was drinking again.

If he did drink again, I think I need to end it. It's not just the drinking itself, it's the unreliable person he becomes when he drinks. My dad is an alcoholic, too, so I have an unhealthy fear of people who drink too much. I know Hunter would never become violent like my dad, but the whole alcoholic boyfriend thing is not going to work for me unless he stays sober.

By the time ten o'clock rolls around and nobody has heard from

Natalie or Hunter, an assistant director comes onto the set and tells us all to go home.

I drive home feeling as if I'm going to barf.

I'm already in bed, when Oscar comes and knocks.

"You okay?" he asks. I know he was there on set somewhere the whole time, too.

I shrug. "What the fuck?"

He sighs loudly. "I know. But they found them."

I'm not sure I want to hear this but I wait.

"Natalie apparently started drinking. Hunter didn't know it, but when they got to the AA meeting, she went in the bathroom and drank. He couldn't tell until she started driving them back to the set."

"She was driving?"

"Hunter talked her into pulling over. She did and ran to the edge of a cliff and sat there saying she was going to jump. She had both of their cell phones and threw them down into the water."

"Well that explains why he didn't call me back."

"I guess he spent the entire time trying to convince her not to kill herself. Be easy on him, Kennedy, he's a wreck."

I narrow my eyes. "How do you know all this?"

"I was in Brock's office when Hunter came in with Natalie. She could barely walk. He somehow talked her into getting off the cliff and he didn't know what to do with her so he went straight to his dad. Liza took her straight to the bathroom because she was puking all over the place. While she was gone, Hunter explained."

"Why are you the one telling me this instead of him?" I say.

Oscar squirms and shrugs. "I'm sure it's because he's with his dad. When I left him he was in the car with his dad. They are driving Natalie to the Palm Springs detox center. The film is on hiatus for at least two weeks."

"Hunter had to go, too?"

"I think Natalie wouldn't go unless he came."

"Fucking fantastic," I say.

"Hey, kiddo, I know it sucks. I just wanted to tell you right away."

I nod. Oscar stands there. "Okay," I say. "Thanks for letting me know."

"Kennedy," he says before he leaves. "I'm sure if Hunter had a phone he would've called you and told you. And I doubt he can talk right now with her in the car. Not to mention his dad."

"Yeah," I say, "you're probably right."

But I wonder.

12

I sleep in the next day. When I wake, I check my phone.

There is a message from Hunter. I don't recognize the number, but I can see the first word says, "Boots"—his nickname for me—so I open it.

"Crazy night. I'm in Palm Springs. This is my number for a while. A burner phone. My cell is gone. In the Pacific Ocean somewhere I guess. Call me when you wake up. So much to say."

I immediately dial him and it goes to voice mail.

"Hey. Oscar gave me the skinny. When do you get to come home?" I say then at the last minute I add, "Sounds like you had a rough time last night." Then I hang up.

Oscar said he was in rough shape and a wreck from trying to talk Natalie out of jumping. I wonder if that bitch knows that suicidal girls are his Achilles heel? His long-time girlfriend, Carly, controlled him for a long time with her suicide attempts and threats.

Déjà vu?

I laze around the house most of the day. Oscar sleeps in and then goes to the gym. My mom must've headed to work before I woke up.

But she calls around ten.

"Hi, honey," she says. "Oscar told me what happened. I didn't want to wake you on a rare day when you can sleep in."

"Thanks, mom," I say.

Then she is quiet and I'm suddenly worried.

She exhales loudly before she speaks. "Your dad's appeal was granted."

My face grows icy cold and I feel like I'm going to faint. The room is spinning. I grip the kitchen counter.

"Kennedy?"

"What does that mean?"

"It means he's going to be released."

"But you guys are still divorced, right?"

"Oh, god, yes, honey. He's not going to be a part of our lives in any way. That is unless you want him to be?"

"No fucking way."

"Kennedy."

"Sorry for swearing but it's true. No way."

"I respect that," she says and it makes me suddenly wary.

"You feel the same way, right, mom?"

"Absolutely," she says. "I have no desire to ever see him again. I wrote him a letter forgiving him and now that chapter in my life is over. I don't have to think about it anymore."

I can feel the relief surge through me. "Thank God."

"Well, I'll let you get back to your day off, sweetie. I think we should go out to dinner tonight, I miss you. That is, unless you have plans with Hunter?"

"I miss you, too, mom," I say. "Let's make it a date."

We hang up before I say anything about why Hunter and I don't have plans.

For all I know he's driving home from Palm Springs right now but he hasn't bothered to let me know. If he thinks I'm sitting around all day not making plans for tonight in case he shows up or calls, he's wrong.

In fact, part of me secretly hopes he shows up tonight and I'm gone. Serves him right.

With the house to myself, I grab a book and head to our deck overlooking the beach. I sprawl in a lounge chair and drink ice tea and read for hours. Hunter still hasn't called back.

I'm a little sick to my stomach about my dad being out on appeal. Despite my mom's nonchalance about it, I'm scared. And I want to talk to Hunter about it. I want him to hug me and tell me it's going to be okay. Because I need to act strong for my mom.

Finally, around two my phone rings.

"Hey," he says in a low, husky voice.

Despite myself, his voice makes me melt.

"Hey, yourself," I say and smile.

"Kennedy, the past twenty-four hours have been nuts."

"Sounds like it," I say lightly and then close my mouth. It's up to him to talk.

He tells me basically what Oscar had relayed and then says, "On our way to the meeting the other day her boyfriend sent her a text. He was dumping her. I guess she couldn't take it."

"So, she decided to drink and try to kill herself?" I say, in a somewhat cold tone.

"Yeah," he says and sighs loudly. "But I think she'll be okay now that she's here. She's hungover but ready to start working the program."

"That's good," I say.

"Yeah." But then he doesn't say anything else. What's left unsaid is bothering me and he hasn't answered me about when he's coming home.

Finally, I say, "So I guess your dad has us on hiatus for at least two weeks for her work the program. It sucks, but I'm glad because I'll actually get to see you again on more than the weekends."

He clears his throat and I feel panic race over me. I know what he's going to say is going to be bad.

"About that," he says and pauses. "Um, so she's really needy and insecure and doesn't really have any friends—"

"Gee, I wonder why," I interrupt in a sarcastic tone. I don't want him to keep talking. I know whatever he says is going to change everything.

"And so, she asked me to be her sponsor."

"What the fuck does that mean?"

"It means she calls me when she wants to drink and stuff and I talk to her about it," he says.

"I know what a sponsor is. What does that mean if you're her sponsor?" I ask. "I mean I know you call up your sponsor Randy when you are having a bad day or feel like you want to have a drink, right?"

"Yeah. Same thing. Except," he says.

"Except what, Hunter?"

"Um, it looks like I'm going to stay here too for the two weeks."

I close my eyes and don't answer. In the distances, I can hear little kids screaming and splashing in the waves and a dog barking and a cheer come up at a nearby beach volleyball game.

"Boots?"

"What do you want me to say, Hunter?"

"I want you to say you love me and understand."

"I love you."

"Okay," he says after a few seconds. "I guess I'll take that for now."

"Call me when you're ready to come home."

I hang up.

And then I sit and cry. I feel like a baby. I know I'm feeling sorry for myself. But while Hunter is babysitting and taking care of another girl, I'm his girlfriend and I need him.

I wanted to tell him about my dad's appeal. I needed to talk to him about it. But apparently, this movie star bitch is too important and is going to get all his attention.

The jealousy makes me double over holding my stomach. He's my boyfriend. Not hers. I need him.

Thinking this reminds me of one day last winter when I was feeling really sick. I needed my mom. She was always there for me when I was sick, but she hadn't moved out here yet. And even if Oscar hadn't been busy on the set I would've felt odd turning to him.

But I needed someone. I felt like death warmed over.

I hadn't slept, not really, the night before because my head and neck and face hurt so bad with whatever flu or crap had knocked me out. I hadn't showered in two days. My hair was sticking up everywhere. When I used the bathroom, I was afraid to look in the mirror. I had black bags under my eyes and wan skin. I had managed to brush my teeth once, but that was about it.

After texting me for two days and me telling him to stay away so he wouldn't catch the plague I had, on the third day Hunter decided he was coming anyway, if I liked it or not.

He showed up with some Pho soup from a restaurant I liked and after I managed to drink some of it, I just moaned. I felt like a baby, but I couldn't help it.

"What hurts?" he asked.

"Everything. My legs, my throat, my head, but mostly around my eyes and nose," I said.

"Scoot up," he said. I did and he crawled in bed behind me with his back resting on the headboard. Then he piled pillows in his lap and had me lay my head there. Then, from above and behind, he started massaging my face and head and neck.

"Oh, my God," I breathed. "I'm never going to leave you."

He laughed. "Is it helping?"

"It's the first time I haven't been in pain for two days. So yeah."

"Good."

Then he sat there for at least a half hour gently massaging my face and neck and running his fingers lightly through my hair until I felt like I had melted into the pillow.

Then, I must've fallen asleep. I woke and was disoriented. Then I remembered. Hunter was still sitting behind me in the dark.

I sat up. "Hunter?"

"You feel better?"

"A little, yeah. Thanks. How long was I asleep?"

"Forty-five minutes maybe?"

"And you just sat there the whole time?"

"I know you've been having trouble sleeping and I didn't want to wake you."

He got out of bed and was stretching and making a face.

"You okay?"

"Just got a leg cramp, it's all good."

That's when I knew that Hunter really truly loved me. I mean I knew before, but that was proof solid.

And right now, I know that if I reached out to him and told him I needed him more than Natalie needed him, he would drop everything and come to me.

I thought about it long and hard. And ultimately decided not to call him.

He was mine.

And one thing I loved about him was how he cared for his friends so deeply.

Even if I didn't like the so-called friend.

It was who he was. And I would accept it.

13

A week passes. Hunter and I speak every day.

He asks me once if I'm okay with him being gone.

"I don't like it," I say.

"I don't, either."

"I'm a little jealous," I finally say. "Natalie gets all of you and I get none of you."

"She gets my help," he says without skipping a beat. "You get my heart."

It's a good answer. It helps me keep my jealousy in check.

I try to keep busy during this hiatus. I've bought some of the books I'm going to need for my classes in the fall and am getting a head start on some of the work. As a film major, a lot of the assignments also involved watching and analyzing famous movies.

I spend each afternoon in the home movie theater with a pad of paper taking notes and rewinding movies.

One day Hunter calls me and sounds excited.

"I think there's a good chance I'll be home soon," he says. "Natalie is doing really well. She says she never wants to drink again and wants to be back on the set filming. She's bored out of her mind here."

I don't give a shit about Natalie, I want to say. But her moods and emotions and behaviors are infuriatingly tied to my boyfriend now and when I can next see him. And the last thing I want to do is be a jealous girlfriend. It only makes me look bad.

I'm not stupid. I know girls get cheated on all the time. Hunter's not perfect. But I choose to believe him and trust him.

Plus, if he is cheating on me with her—which I sincerely doubt— I'll eventually find out and can deal with it then. Until then I am going to be the trusting girlfriend. Jealous girlfriends only make themselves look bad.

My attitude is if he doesn't want me, I don't want him. And I mean it.

But let's face it, I hope he *does* want me.

Because I want him. And I can't wait to see him in person so I can tell him about my dad. I know I could've told him over the phone but I really need to tell him in person. I want him to hold me if I break down. For so many years of my life I was strong and independent because I had to be: because my mom had enough to worry about with my dad without also having to worry about me.

So now, sometimes it feels good to need someone else, or even to just lean on someone for support.

I don't think it makes me any less strong to admit this.

"I can't wait to see you," I say. "I hope you're right."

"I'll know more tomorrow," he says. "Maybe I can even come home tomorrow night."

"That would be great," I say, trying to match his enthusiasm.

THE NEXT DAY Hunter calls and I can tell by the tone of his voice that he's down.

"Natalie saw some picture of her ex with some model and now she's on a hunger strike and they said no way she's leaving yet."

"How convenient," I say and instantly regret being snarky.

But Hunter surprises me and says, "I know."

He's opened the door so I say, "Hunter do you really have to be there? Do you really have to be her sponsor?"

He's quiet for a moment and then says, "My dad says that if this film flops we are going to be out more than a million dollars." His voice lowers to a whisper. "There's something to do with financing and the studio is pressuring my dad to get this one done on budget and that's why he's accommodating everything she asks. And because I'm his son, I have to help, Kennedy. I know you are being unbelievably cool and understanding about this and I am really grateful for that."

I swallow back my tears. Finally, he's acknowledged how shitty this is for me.

"It's just," I say and stop when my voice breaks. "I need you, too," I finally say in a low voice.

"I know," he says. "I feel the same. This is really starting to get me down. I thought I wanted to be a sponsor, but it's a lot harder than I thought."

It doesn't cost me any effort to say, "Hang in there. I'm proud of you."

We hang up both feeling sad and down.

14

The next day everything falls apart.

My mom is at work. Oscar is somewhere. And there is a knock on the door.

I open it thinking it's the pizza I ordered.

But it's my dad.

He's standing on the front porch. I nearly slam the door. My heart is racing and I feel faint.

The last time I saw him I hit him in the head with a baseball bat.

Last year, Hunter did a film project interviewing me about my childhood and I told him all my secrets.

"My grandmother died around the same time my dad got fired from the fire department for drinking. It started a vicious downward spiral," I say. I pause. I know I sound formal and detached as I describe what happened, reciting clichés. I inhale deeply. "It was the beginning of the end."

"Explain," Hunter says.

"The more he drank, the more violent he got. He never hit me, but he started hitting my mom. And my whole world fell apart," I say.

I'd shared most of this with a therapist in the fall. And Hunter knew the basic story, but this felt different, harder.

"*My mom didn't really try to stop him. I mean she probably did, but it didn't seem like it to me. It seemed like she just put up with it.*"

"*It seems like you might be angry at her for that?*"

I look up and blink. I process that for a few seconds. "Yeah. Yeah, I guess I am."

"*You want to talk more about that?*"

"*One day last year, I came home and my dad was beating up my mom. I mean he'd hit her before and then apologized and cried to both of us, but this time was different. This time he didn't stop. He was kicking her while she was on the ground. I had to hit him over the head with a baseball bat to stop him.*"

The camera instantly drops. Hunter is wide-eyed, his mouth open.

I shrug. "*Yeah. There you have it.*"

I go on to tell him how I called 911. How both my parents were taken to the hospital and the police officer took me to my friend Sherie's house because I had no other family. And how when my dad was checked out and determined to be fine from my attack, he was arrested and transferred to jail. And I came to live with Oscar while my mother was recovering in a long-term facility.

And now here he is again. He looks different and yet the same. I hate him. And I love him. But more than anything I wish I could close my eyes and he would disappear.

"Hi, Kennedy," he says and looks down at his feet. "Can I come in?"

He looks a lot older than when I saw him a year ago. His hair is all gray now and cut short. He is a lot skinnier. He wears jeans and a button up flannel shirt and boots. His eyes have bags under them and crow's feet.

"I don't know," I say. I look over his shoulder to see if he drove a car here but there are no unfamiliar cars parked in the driveway. Shit.

"Okay. That's fair," he says. Then he turns toward the porch. "Can we talk out here?"

My heart is beating double time and I feel like I'm going to faint. But I manage to nod. I step out and pull the door closed behind me. We stand there awkwardly.

Finally, he clears his throat. "I came because I wanted to make amends to you in person."

"Okay," I say. I'm reluctant to give him an inch. He nearly beat my mom to death.

"I don't expect you to forgive me," he says. "In fact, part of me hopes you don't so that will be part of my punishment. But I also know that forgiveness is for you, not me. So, for that reason alone I hope you will consider it."

I don't answer.

He keeps talking. "I also came to tell you I love you. For what it's worth. I did some things, a lot of things, that are completely unforgivable. I know that you will probably be affected by the terrible things I've done for your entire life and I will never ever forgive myself for that. You and your mom didn't deserve any of the awful things I did."

"Don't say her name," I say coldly.

He looks up. "Okay."

Then he looks away again and keeps talking. "But I know now that alcohol turns me into a different person. I'm not using that as excuse, I'm just stating a fact. But I'm never, ever going to take another drink again. And I've been in anger management classes and I can control my temper now, too."

I want to cry. And I'm sick of hearing what he has to say. I put my hand on the door.

"Can you please just leave now?" I say and my voice is shaking. I need him gone before I break down crying. "You've said what you wanted to say. Can you please just leave?"

He nods. I open the door.

"Just so you know," he says. "I'll order a car but I might be out here a few seconds until it gets here."

"Okay," I say wearily. But I pause. He looks up, hopefully and then his face falls at my words.

"If you love me like you say, promise me you won't ever come to this house again?"

He looks at me and then nods solemnly. "I promise."

I close the door and go inside, suddenly feeling like I'm a hundred years old.

My entire body is shaking madly. I'm so confused.

I don't really hate my dad. I almost feel sorry for him. I feel sorry that I can't love him anymore.

He's tried to kill himself twice. Once after he was arrested and once when he was sentenced. A small part of me wonders if me rejecting him now will make him try to kill himself again. I would die. I don't want him dead. I just don't want him to show up at my house. He hurt us too badly. I don't think I can ever trust him again.

I peek out the side window. He's smoking a cigarette and pacing. It seems like he's careful not to look up at the house or windows. I get the feeling he's doing that for me. I spy on him until I see a car come and take him away.

Only then do I collapse on the couch. Everything feels upside down. I never expected to see my dad again and then he shows up here, at my home. At the first place I've felt safe at in years.

Suddenly Oscar's home doesn't feel safe anymore. I head to my room and lock the door. I crawl under the covers and just feel numb.

What I want more than anything is to talk to Hunter about it, but he's too busy being there for another girl.

I can't talk to my mom about it. Not right away. I don't want her to get upset or worry about me anymore. I mean, yeah, I'll tell her my dad came, but I won't let her know how it's flattened me and sent me to bed.

But right then the last thing in the world I want is to tell my mom that my dad showed up on our front porch. He promised he wouldn't come back.

Maybe I'm a fool but I believe him. If he truly loves me and wants my forgiveness as he says, he wouldn't dare fuck me over any more than he already has, would he?

15

Ava and I meet again. This time at a little coffee shop in Venice on Saturday morning. Since Hunter is babysitting in Palm Springs, I don't have any plans.

"I don't know how to get him back," Ava says, playing with the straw of her iced macchiato. "I've thought of so many ways but all of them would end up screwing us over later."

"Like what?" I say and take a bite of my croissant.

"Like cutting off his dick."

"Yeah. We would definitely mess up our own lives if we did that," I say.

She lifts an eyebrow. "Might be worth it, though?"

I start to laugh. Crumbs from my croissant go everywhere.

Then she laughs.

Pretty soon we are leaning over holding our stomachs and laughing so hard we're crying.

"I was thinking," I say. "You did a pretty damn good job doctoring that video in Josh's favor..."

She looks down and her face flushes.

"And we both know a lot about video and film, right?"

Now she looks up and nods.

"I think our revenge should come in the form of a short film."

She raises an eyebrow.

"You said you didn't think police would believe you because of your record, right?"

She nods.

"But if three girls come forward, they'd have to believe it."

She nods seriously. "I like what you're thinking."

"It might be risky."

"I'm in," she says.

"Here's what I was thinking," I begin.

16

After the coffee shop, we head into L.A. and stop at a store that sells spy gear.

Ava spends $500 on our gear. I offer to help pay and she puts out her palm, "Let me get this to make up for my role in everything."

I nod my thanks.

Then we go back to my house and test everything out.

Once we are pretty sure it works, Ava texts Josh.

"I miss you. I'm horny."

"Blunt," I say.

"It'll work," she says. "Because his ego is so big and he thinks with his cock, he'll bite, hook, line and sinker."

She's right.

He texts back right away. "I'm having a party at my house tonight. The parents are out of town. Come early so I can take care of you properly. Six?"

"Deal," she writes back.

Then she leans back and takes a big breath. "We're on."

"You okay with all this?" I ask.

"Yeah," she says, her eyes gleaming. "I'm more than ready."

"I'll be close by," I remind her."

17

At fifteen minutes to six, I'm parked in the driveway of the neighbor's house with my laptop and cell phone set up on the passenger seat. My ear pods are connected to the laptop program.

When we devised our plan earlier, Ava had told me the family next door spent summers in the south of France on their yacht and so the house was empty. All I need is the driveway.

"I'm pulling in," Ava says in my ear.

I can't reply to her. She trusts me to be there.

I switch on the live feed on my laptop and see Josh's house from her viewpoint. The camera lens on her sunglasses record smoothly and it's as if I'm right there with her as she gets out of her car and takes a path that leads around the back of the house. There is a small guest house set back near an area with large trees. She opens the door. It is dimly lit but I can make out Josh spread eagle on the bed. He's naked and fondling himself.

"There is the woman of the hour," he says. "Right on time."

"That's right, Josh."

He sits up slightly.

"What's up with the nerd glasses?" he asks.

"I thought maybe you needed a visit from the naughty librarian."

He chuckles. "Oh, yeah, I do. Big time!"

I don't know how she does it without wanting to barf, but she is a good actress, that's for sure.

"Get your clothes off now," he says with a growl.

"Easy, tiger," she says confidently. "I think we need to talk about how we left things first."

"I don't want to talk," he says like a pouty toddler.

"I know, but if you want me to fully pleasure you without any resentment, I have a few things to get off my chest," she says, smoothly. "Just let me say my piece and then I have big, big plans for you."

He sits up. "I like the sound of that."

Then her voice softens.

"Josh, I still have an issue with you setting me up with the football team," she says. "I mean, you didn't even ask if I wanted to have sex with all of them. You never approached me first. You don't know what I would have said. For all you know I might have said yes and then I could've enjoyed it, but it was hard to enjoy it when they were all forcing themselves on me."

He scowls. "I don't want to talk about that. We're wasting time talking."

"I need to get it off my chest if we are going to have an ongoing sexual relationship. I hope you understand? Isn't that what you want, Josh? I want to be fuck buddies. I want us to have sex whenever one of us is feeling horny and in order to do that I need to clear the air."

Damn, she's good.

I sit back watching the live footage on my laptop and marveling at her composure.

Josh sighs loudly. "Fine."

"You didn't have to drug me to get the football players to have sex with me. And you didn't need to beat me. I wasn't going to say anything."

Now Josh leaps off the bed and looks around wildly. "What the fuck, Ava? Why are you even talking about this?" He's clearly agitated and is pacing. "Do we have to keep talking about that night?"

"Okay," she says in a conciliatory tone. "I've said my piece about that. Let's move on."

"There's more?" He rolls his eyes and reaches for her breasts. She backs up.

"It's about the video with Kennedy," she says.

I'm holding my breath now.

"Jesus!" Josh says.

"Listen," Ava says. "I'm scared to death that they are going to figure out I doctored that video tape with Kennedy on it. If they do, I could go to jail."

"So?"

"So?" she shrieks.

"I didn't do anything to her anyway," he says.

"But you would've," Ava says.

He shrugs. "She wanted it anyway."

"Not from what I saw."

"It didn't mean anything. I just was gonna fuck her. She would've thanked me afterward. She thought she didn't want it, but once she had me, she'd have changed her mind."

"That doesn't make me feel better," Ava says.

He cocks his head. "You jealous? Don't be? You're the one I care about."

"But she didn't want to—have sex with you. I saw that."

"That bitch deserves for me to fuck her brains out if she wants it or not. I thought you hated her as much as I do? What's all this about, Ava?"

My heart is pounding. He's getting suspicious.

She reaches for him and caresses his junk. He smiles. "That's more like it."

"Oh!" she says loudly and backs off. "I forgot. I got us some X!"

His grin widens. "Fuck yeah. That's my Ava."

She extracts a small piece of plastic and extracts two pills from it. She says, "Open up," and reaches for his mouth. He opens his mouth and she places it on his tongue. Then she pretends to eat hers. Or at least that was the plan. I only see her hand move up to her mouth.

It's actually X. Ava had to hit up her old drug dealer to get one. She thought about slipping Josh a Roofie, but it would take too long to work so she got some Ketamine to put in his drink. It can start affecting someone in one to thirty minutes.

He pulls her to him and kisses her. At last that's what I assume. All I see is blurry pink on the screen.

She pulls back.

"Let's have a drink since it will take a while for the X to work," she says and takes out some vodka and soda. She heads over to his desk where there are red plastic cups. Ava fixes a drink and hands him one. But she slips some liquid into his glass as she fixes his with the ketamine.

We are going to blur or just cut this out of the video we plan to hand over to the police. Even though you can hear what's happening she won't be in trouble for handing him an X pill and him willingly swallowing it. The ketamine, however, is another story.

I'm holding my breath, afraid he's going to see and say something. But when she turns back around, he's spread eagle on the bed again playing with himself. What's up with that?

She hands him her drink and then tilts her own back. He downs his instantly and she smiles.

"Want more?"

He reaches for you. "I want you."

"Patience. Let's wait for the X to kick in. Sex on X is the best thing ever."

"Ugh," he says.

"I'll go freshen up. I've got a surprise for you. Something pretty to wear I thought you might like. Goes with my librarian glasses." She grabs her tote bag and heads for the bathroom. In the bathroom, she is looking at the mirror. Her face is red. I know she's stressing out.

I hear Josh call for her from the other room, but it sounds sleepy and incoherent.

Ava stares at the mirror and counts to twenty.

Then she takes a deep breath and opens the bedroom door.

Josh is lying with his eyes closed on the bed. "Josh?" she says in a soft voice. He sort of mumbles and his eyes are half slits.

"Don't feel so good."

"I'll be right back," she says. She grabs her bag and runs out.

A few minutes later she's in the van with me and we are going over the footage.

"You fucking did it!" I say.

"I did, didn't I?" she says, sounding surprised. "An eye for an eye, bitch. Drug me? I'll drug you."

"That was pretty brave," I say. "I was nervous for you a couple times."

She nods.

"Okay," I say. "Let's go back to my place and edit the rest of the film."

Ava stays the night, sleeping in the spare bedroom downstairs so we can get an early start the next day.

18

Reno

Tammy Kohl is a pretty girl with long brown hair and giant brown eyes. She's unusually skinny though, all knees and elbows. And she is shaking when she walks over to our table at the casino's restaurant.

The place isn't open yet, but Tammy works there and arranged for us to go take up a corner booth and film.

"Thanks for coming," I say.

She nods. "Anything to make that bastard pay."

"My sentiments, exactly," Ava says.

When we emailed her we basically told her our stories, but we go over it again and our plan, including what we did last night.

"We are pretty good with what we already have," I say, "But it would make it even stronger with your story."

She nods coolly.

"I'm in."

I point the camera toward her.

Then she shares with us how Josh Masters sexually assaulted her and then threatened her when she went to the police. Apparently, Josh Master's father paid her lowlife stepfather $50,000 to convince her not to go to the police. The stepfather worked for Josh's dad. So, it was a combination of paying him off and threatening to fire him, Tammy says.

Her mother said they needed the money so they didn't lose their house and so Tammy agreed. But then her mother divorced her stepdad and they got an apartment anyway. She's regretted dropping the charges ever since.

"I was so worried he would do it to someone else," she says. "And I was right."

Now she is crying. "It's all my fault. If I would've been brave I could've stopped him and he would never have been able to do those things to you two."

I reach out and put my hand on her. "I totally understand why you did what you did," I say. "Anyone else would've done the same thing as you did."

She looks at me like she really wants to believe me.

Ava nods. "He's a monster. He's manipulative and he's evil and it's all going to stop right now with the three of us, right?"

Tammy nods. We all hold hands and look at each other fiercely.

Ava and I stay up most of the night editing in Oscar's home theater.

When my mom and him peek in, we tell them it's a secret project that we want to show them before it goes public, but aren't ready yet.

They both smile.

If they only knew.

Once we finish the video, Ava crashes in the spare bedroom at dawn and I crawl into my bed.

We wake at two and she leaves.

"Thanks," she says.

"It's not over yet."

"See you for the grand finale Friday."

I nod.

This Friday it's outdoor movie night at the beach. It's an annual tradition for the students at Pacific High to spend the Friday night closest to the Fourth of July at Balboa Beach and the night kicks off with an outdoor movie projected on the concrete wall of the snack bar.

One of Ava's father's friends is in charge of showing the movie and he's agreed to play our little expose first as a preview.

It's always an R rated movie so we don't have to worry about kids seeing our preview.

All of this has kept me so busy I've pushed back all thoughts of my dad and his visit. And Hunter.

Hunter has texted a few times. I haven't even told him about the Josh revenge plan. Part of me is worried he'll try to stop me. Or that he'll be upset because he doesn't trust Ava. I feel guilty not telling him, but I know it's the right thing.

And still, my dad was here.

On Thursday morning, in a weak moment, I text Hunter. "Wish I could talk to you in person. There's a lot going on here. It's a long story, but my dad showed up at my house. He got out on appeal."

I hit send and wait. He doesn't reply. I swallow back my tears. Fuck it. I'm on my own.

But I do need to tell my mom.

She's out so I have to wait until she gets home. She has the day off, but I don't know where she is.

Finally, she walks in.

She looks like she's been crying and alarm zings through me.

"Mom?"

She smiles through her tears. "I'm sorry. I just had breakfast with your dad. He's in town. He called me earlier this week."

I have a giant lump in my throat suddenly.

"Did he tell you he showed up here?"

Her eyes widen in alarm. "No!" she says and stands. I can tell she's pissed off. "That is not okay. I told him that I would ask you if you were ready to see him and he agreed not to contact you until I got back to him."

"This was the other day."

Her eyes narrow. And she shakes her head and presses her lips tightly together. "I'm so sorry."

I shrug. But then she comes and wraps me in her arms and I cry.

"Why didn't you tell me?"

I shake my head. "I don't know. I guess I felt like if I didn't say it out loud it wasn't real."

"Oh, honey," she says and hugs me tighter.

We sit on the edge of her bed as she holds me and I weep. She is holding me and telling me that everything is going to be okay. When I finally can catch my breath, I try to talk.

"I want to hate him so much, mama," I say. I haven't called her mama since I was little.

"I know, honey. I know," she says soothingly.

"I don't know if I'm ready to see him or let him be my dad."

"It's okay. You do whatever feels best for you," she says. "I met with him and then decided what is best for me is to not see him again. It's too painful. He agreed. He's flying back Saturday afternoon. He's available for breakfast in the morning if you decide to see him."

I don't answer.

"It would just be at a restaurant close by, somewhere neutral. It's up to you. You are almost eighteen, Kennedy, and I respect whatever you decide."

"How long until I have to decide?" I ask.

She shrugs. "I guess until he has to leave for the airport on Saturday."

I nod and sniff. "Okay."

Then I tell her about our secret project about Josh.

She listens intently and then starts to cry.

I grab her hand. "Mom? Why are you crying?"

"I'm just so sorry this happened to you and proud of the way you three girls are handling it. All on your own."

"We're going to need Oscar's help getting this in the right hands."

"Of course! We'll tell him as soon as he gets home from work."

Oscar is back on the set. They are filming some small scenes without Natalie. But the rest of us are still on hiatus until Monday.

19

W hen Oscar gets home, we all head downstairs and I
show them the film Ava and I made in the home
theater.

My mom cries more.

Oscar stands and paces.

"I'm not a violent man, but I want to hurt that boy."

I've never seen Oscar angry like this.

"Me too," my mom says. "But Kennedy's way is right."

Oscar nods. Before we go to bed, he takes his copy of the film and locks it up in his safe.

It's reassuring, but also makes me nervous.

I'M in a deep sleep dreaming of my phone ringing incessantly when I finally climb out of my fog and realize it really is ringing.

I look down at it.

Hunter.

"Hello?" I say huskily.

"I'm here."

"What?"

"I'm out front. It's cold. Can you come let me in?"

"Kay."

I'm still half sleep walking when I stumble down the stairs and open the door. And there he is.

He gives me the sweetest smile and I can't help but smile back.

I jump into his arms. "God, I missed you."

"I missed you more," he says.

We settle on the couch in the living room and catch up.

"I'm sorry I haven't been good about keeping in touch. Being someone's sponsor is a nightmare. I'm not ready for it. I actually quit."

"What?"

"Yeah. As soon as I got your text—about your dad—I quit. I needed to be here for you. With you. But I had to finish up some things the rest of the day, though or I would've been here sooner."

"Wow."

"Natalie is too needy. I want to be a good friend, but she doesn't just want a friend, she wants a manservant or something."

I close my mouth. There is no use saying, "I told you so."

"Think she's going to say sober?"

He nods. "Yeah. I think that the whole boyfriend thing sent her backsliding but she realizes now that she can't let someone else affect her well-being and her future."

"Well that's good."

But then I grab his face. "I don't really want to talk about Natalie."

"God, I'm sorry," he says. "Tell me what happened with your dad?"

"There's not much to tell. I mean my interaction with him was less than five minutes. It's just the whole thing about how I felt after. Like how I feel about him being out of prison and thinking he can just come into our lives again."

But then it all spills out and I tell him exactly how it went down with me and my dad. What I said. What my dad said. How I feel. And that he went to breakfast with my mom and wants to go to breakfast with me on Saturday.

"Wow, that's rough," he says.

We sit there quietly for a few seconds.

"You going to meet him for breakfast?"

I shrug. "I don't know. Probably not."

"Do you think you'll ever be able to forgive him?" he asks.

"I don't know." And I mean it. I really don't know.

"I didn't think I could ever forgive my mom, either," he says.

"I know. And that makes me so happy. Seeing you guys together and the love you have for each other ... it's really great."

"Yeah," he says smiling.

"I just don't know," I say. "I mean I'm not saying the situation with your mom is easier than what I have with my dad, but your mom didn't physically beat you or your dad up."

"True."

"I just don't know if I can forgive him."

"I get that," he says. "Believe me, I do. And I know this sounds cliché, but remember that you forgive someone for you, not for them."

"So, I've heard," I say. It's a constant theme. One, that frankly, I'm pretty sick of hearing. I don't want to forgive my dad for me. Or for him. It feels too right to hold onto that hate and anger. It feels like by doing so, I'm keeping myself safe. That it will keep me from getting hurt more or again. But deep down inside I know this is a lie.

Hunter draws me in for a tight hug.

"I know whatever you decide will be the right thing," he says.

He starts to kiss my neck and grabs my hips pulling me toward him. And for the first time in our relationship, I push him away. My touch is gentle, but it's still the first time I've rejected him.

"I need to get some sleep," I say. "Thanks for coming home for me."

He leans down and kisses my forehead. "Can I tuck you in? I can let myself out."

I'm a little suspicious that he's going to try to talk me into sex after all once we're in my room, but he walks me to my bedroom and pulls the covers up to my chin and then kisses me softly, says, "Sleep well," turns out the light, and is gone.

∼

THE NEXT DAY I see on Twitter that Natalie and her rock star boyfriend are back together.

I text Hunter. "Are you only home because Natalie's boyfriend kicked you out?" I know it's mean.

"What? No. I didn't even know that. I came because you told me your dad was here."

"Oh."

He writes "?"

And I say, "Thanks again."

"Yeah."

Hunter is at my place the next day around eleven. Oscar and my mom are just getting ready to leave the house to take a copy of my video to the D.A.'s office. They said I don't have to be there.

I had texted Hunter and told him we needed to talk.

"Is it bad?" he had said.

"Only for Josh Masters."

"See you soon."

When Hunter walks in I hug my mom and Oscar goodbye.

My mom says, "You did the right thing, Kennedy." She smiles at me and leaves and Hunter raises and eyebrow.

I pour him some coffee with creamer and refill my own.

"Let's go sit on the deck and I'll explain."

The day is gorgeous the way only Los Angeles days can me. The seagulls are flying around above us, the waves crashing on the sand before us, people running by with dogs in tow, little kids splashing in the waves.

I breathe it all in deeply and then turn to Hunter.

"Ava came to me and told me some things,"

He sets down his mug of coffee and looks alarmed.

"Josh hurt her even worse than me. And we know what he did to Dex. So, we made a little plan."

Hunter's eyes get wide. "What plan?"

I tell him everything.

"Holy shit you were busy while I was gone," is all he says when I finish.

"Oscar thinks this the video is enough to get an arrest warrant."

Hunter shakes his head. "Wow. Wow. I don't know what to say."

I shrug. "Me, either. The last person I thought I would collaborate with is Ava."

Hunter nods. "She's a little messed up, but she's not that bad. At least the Ava I knew growing up wasn't that bad. She's got a chip on her shoulder now for sure, though."

I stare at him for a second and then the realization strikes me and I say it out loud. "She's my friend now."

He holds up both palms. "Fine. Just be careful."

"I know," I say. "Speaking of Ava, I need to figure out when and where to meet her. We want to show up at the movie night together."

I pick up my phone to text Ava. We tried to get Tammy to come down from Reno, but she said she had to work.

Ava doesn't text me back.

Hunter and I go to brunch and I send her three more texts. The last one says, "I'm worried. You okay?"

After brunch, Hunter drops me off to head home for a few hours.

Shortly after he leaves, I call Liza's personal cell.

"I'm sorry, Liza, I'm quitting. I appreciate the opportunity, but I only have a few weeks until college starts and I need to prepare."

It feels a little spontaneous, but in the back of my mind I've been thinking about doing so for a while. I want to enjoy some of my summer before I begin college. I'm not really learning anything to do with filmmaking. I'm a grunt gopher. And that's fine. It's got a purpose—to make connections and to get a feel for the movie life. But I need a break.

I can always work next summer.

"I get it, kid," she says. "Keep my number. You can use it as a reference. You are one of the few P.A.'s I've worked with who always has grace under pressure. We can use more of that on movie sets."

I hang up, smiling. Grace under pressure, huh? Who knew?

Earlier, I'd told Hunter what I was going to do. I asked if his dad would think badly of me.

"Nah. That dude is so busy and wrapped up in his own world, he probably won't even notice. No offense to you, of course."

"None taken."

Meanwhile, I keep texting and calling Ava, getting increasingly alarmed. She should have been in touch by now.

Part of me is scared to death that Josh found out what we are planning and is doing something—or did something–to try to stop her.

And I'm not completely wrong.

At five o'clock, Oscar gets a call from the D.A.

Ava is in the hospital. She was beat up and dumped in an alley. A homeless guy found her and called the police.

We rush to the hospital.

I rush into her room and grab her hand. She has a black eye and a neck brace.

"Oh my, God," I say. "What happened?"

Ava was walking home from the beach when Josh pulled over and forced her into his car. An elderly woman walking her dog saw the whole thing and called 911 giving them the license plate number for Josh's car.

A BOLO went out announcing that she was in danger and a description of Josh's car.

But nobody could find her. Ava said Josh took her to an alley in Venice and beat her up and then left her for dead. He told her he was punishing her for drugging him and leading him on the other night.

Now, the D.A. said, police have an arrest warrant for Josh.

I am squeezing her hand so tightly. "We met with the DA today. He has the film."

She closes her eyes and a tear slips out. "Thank God."

"He says it's good. He says it's going to work. Even if Josh hadn't done this to you, they'd have issued an arrest warrant anyway. He's going away, Ava. He will never hurt us again."

"Thank God," she says and opens her eyes to meet mine.

We were once enemies but now we will be forever bonded in our hatred of Josh Masters. With one look, we can understand what the other is thinking. I know I will do whatever I can to help her if she ever turns to me again.

Then I grow concerned. We'd been so excited about the premiere of our expose but now she's stuck in this hospital bed.

"Should we postpone showing the movie until you get out of here?" I say.

Her eyes narrow. "Oh, hell no. You show that movie, Kennedy. You need to represent. You stand there for all three of us."

The parking lot is jam packed when Hunter and I arrive at the beach

He insisted on driving. And I don't mind. I'm a nervous wreck.

Oscar and my mom will be here somewhere in the crowd a bit later. They say the D.A. told them there will be undercover cops here. In case Josh shows up.

Hunter leads me by the hand through the crowd to where the guy is set up with the projector. He is a skinny guy with long stringy hair and a flannel shirt. He looks like he's in his thirties.

"Robby?" I say.

He looks up from the projector.

"I'm Kennedy," I say.

"Hey," he says. "Ava texted me. We're still good to go. I even asked some of my buddies to hang out near me while it screens in case that douche bag and his buddies try to stop me."

"You're badass, man," Hunter says and fist bumps him. "I can hang out, too, if you need me?"

"Nah, thanks, dude, I'm good with my buddies," he says and nods to a group of guys who look like they are in a motorcycle gang.

"They came just to make sure our film is screened?" I say.

"Yeah."

Without saying a word, I leave and walk over to them. There's four of them with big bushy beards and denim and leather jackets and tattoos. I walk right up to the middle of them.

"I'm Kennedy. I'm one of that guy's victims and I just wanted to thank you for being here. It means a lot to me."

One guy gives me a solemn nod. "We wouldn't miss it for the world," he says. Then he sticks out a thick hand. "I'm Patrick."

"Nice to meet you."

One other guy spits on the ground and cracks his knuckles. "I'm hoping the punk tries to make a move on Robby. I'm just hoping. I don't know Robby's friend's kid, but when I heard that he was still at it even today, I want to beat the little fucker into the pavement. Just give me an excuse."

I nod. "I feel the same. But now that he hurt Ava today there's actually two arrest warrants out for him so just so you know there's going to be some cops undercover around here looking for him. I appreciate you guys being here more than I can say, but I also don't want you to get in trouble for us."

"We're good," the first guy says. "But thanks for the heads up. Much appreciated."

I head back to Hunter and Robby.

There are two chairs set up in front of the projector. Robby gestures to them. "This might be a good spot for you. Especially since my buddies are going to be keeping their eye on the projector. That way if he does show up and threatens you, he won't get far."

Hunter loops his arm around my shoulders. "He'd have to get through me first," he says and I grin that his macho ego has surfaced.

Robby nods. "True that. But the seats will offer a good view."

"That sounds great," I say. "Thanks."

Hunter lifts his arm and soon Devin and Coral and Paige and Dex are there. They sit near us.

Everyone is strangely subdued and quiet. I only just filled them in today on what was going on. There are dozens of people milling around, talking and drinking waiting for the sun to fully set so the movie can be shown.

As soon as it grows dark and Robby flicks on the projector casting a white light on the snack bar wall, everyone moves to take a seat.

Hunter reaches over and grabs my hand. My mouth is suddenly bone dry. My stomach is doing somersaults. I quickly look around to see if there is anybody I recognize. I'm especially alert for Josh's blonde head. I see Robby's motorcycle gang friends flanking the back of us in a semi-circle. It is reassuring.

Then I meet Robby's eyes. He lifts an eyebrow. I nod and squeeze Hunter's hand tightly.

And then it begins.

There is a crackling sound and then there is a picture of the three of us: me, Ava and Tammy up on the wall, larger than life. There is no sound. We are not smiling. Our arms are crossed over our chests. Above our heads are massive words: Josh Masters Assaulted Us: This is our story.

The crowd lets out a collective gasp and then it is dead silent.

But before the interviews with each of us individually, there is a scene with the three of us talking about how he had assaulted all of us at different times and threatened us and then got off scot free.

Then it cuts directly to the footage of Ava talking to him about it. We've blurred out the nudity and didn't show how she drugged him, but the gist of him admitting to what he did is right there.

People are still quiet up to the point where Ava walks into his place and then I hear a commotion. I glance over. It's some members of the football team and some cheerleaders. They are loudly protesting, saying things such as "This is total bullshit." And "This isn't real."

I hear one of the football players, Chad I think saying, "My dad is going to sue the fuck out of you three bitch sluts."

Then I see them. They are starting toward us. Everyone is watching. I'm irritated because people are missing the film. Robby must sense this because he hits pause. The football players heading our way hesitate and then there is a wall made up of the motorcycle gang members.

"You best turn around and go sit your ass down," Patrick says.

Chad makes up some excuse and says something like, "This is bullshit. I'm suing all of you."

The group of football players stalks off.

Robby starts the film again.

The crowd is silent listening to Josh basically admit to everything on film.

Then it immediately cuts to Tammy. She's crying and talking about how Josh assaulted her and then threatened her stepdad's job so she had to drop the charges. She said that she thought it was over because he moved away.

Then Ava's interview shows. She tells how Josh assaulted her the summer before senior year and how he drugged her and made the video.

I hear the football team yelling on the sidelines.

People in the crowd turn to them and tell them to shut the fuck up.

Then two of Robby's motorcycle gang friends head in that direction and soon it is dead quiet again.

Then it's my interview. I talk about how I'm the lucky one. That Hunter stopped him in time.

"God knows how many other attempts were stopped in time," I say. And then I lower my voice, "Or how many other girls out there he assaulted that we just don't know about."

There is a little bit more from me but it is drowned out by yelling and a commotion in the parking lot where the cars are. Everyone stands.

It's Josh. He was running away and an undercover police officer had tackled him and now had him in handcuffs.

I know it's odd, but I run over and get out my camera and film it. Josh looks up at me and says, "You are going to pay you fucking bitch."

Hunter lunges for him, but Devin grabs his arm and stops him.

I say loudly. "This is for you Ava and you Tammy. I wish you could be here to see this. Since you can't I'm capturing it on camera for you because you both deserve to see this monster being taken away in handcuffs like the criminal he is."

Then I turn off my camera and walk away. I'm shaking so hard my teeth are chattering.

Hunter wraps and arm around me and leads me to his Jeep.

"I'm taking you home. I already told your mom and everyone."

I'm too emotionally exhausted to argue.

21

Hunter and I sit on the beach side by side and hold hands watching the sunrise.

The sky is an amazing red shot with pink.

It is the first sunrise I've seen in L.A.

Hunter insisted on picking me up in the dark and armed with two lattes, we spread out a blanket and set up in a good location. To my surprise, we weren't the only ones doing so.

"Unbelievable," I say. I reach for my phone, but then my hand drops. I know this is one of those moments, just like the silver moon on the ocean at night, that can never quite be fully captured on film.

It's the bane of a filmmakers' existence, and yet it also keeps me grounded in the moment, as well.

Hunter has taught me this.

"I can't believe Josh is in jail," I say, unable to stop thinking about the night before.

"Where he belongs," Hunter says.

"Amen."

"You going to be okay testifying this time?" Hunter asks. "I mean without me?"

He smiles.

"I'll manage," I say and smile back. By the time there's a trial, Hunter will already be gone.

Then he clears his throat. "What would you think about maybe sharing an apartment when I get back in February? We could find a place near the campus?"

"Maybe," I say.

"I'll take it."

"I think I'm going to quit my job with my dad," he says. "Dex says he can get me a job working construction for the next three weeks I'm here."

I squint and look at him. "Why?"

"Because my dad thinks I'm his whipping boy and that my job is to babysit Natalie."

"True."

"And I don't think that's the best thing for me and you. I don't like the way she treats you and I'm not going to put up with it. If I have to work with her, I'm going to tell her off and that will just hurt the movie. And it's not like I won't have a million other chances to work on a movie set. Hello! My dad is Brock West."

He pauses for a moment and then says, "Okay. All those reasons are true, but mostly because I want to spend every second of every day with you until I leave so I'm gonna quit."

"Hmmm," I say.

"What's that mean?"

"It means I think that's the best idea I've heard in a long time."

"There's something else I need to tell you," he says and stands. He turns and tugs on both my hands until I'm standing, as well.

Then he drops to his knees before me. And slides a ring on my finger.

"I'm not marrying you, Hunter," I say, mostly joking but a little alarmed. "I'm not even eighteen."

He laughs. "It's a promise ring."

"Oh." I say and smile.

Then he takes both of my hands in his and says, "Kennedy I

promise myself to you and to you only until we see each other again in February. I love you and only want you."

I tug on his hands until he is standing and then I look up at him. "I love you, too. And I promise myself to you back."

"Let's go seal the deal," he says with a smile. "My parents are gone all weekend."

"How about I come by later this afternoon," I say. "I've got something I need to do first."

22

I'm going to go see my dad. I'm scared to death, but it feels like the right thing to do. I have no idea what I am going to say or do, but I know I need to see him before he leaves.

But I'm so full of indecision. I can't make myself call him.

I don't want to sit through a breakfast or lunch. There's no escaping easily if it gets awkward or uncomfortable. My mom says his flight leaves at noon. I'm running out of time.

Finally, at ten, I make a decision.

I'll go see him at the airport. That way if it's awful, he has to get on a plane and leave and I can walk away.

When I tell Hunter and my mom, Hunter insists on driving.

"That way I'll be there for you to talk to right when you get done."

It makes sense so I agree.

Hunter pulls up at the departures.

"I can park and come in if you change your mind," he says.

I smile. "Thanks. But I think I need to do this alone."

"Okay. I'll be right here," he says and squeezes my hand.

"Thanks."

On the drive over, my mom had texted me my dad's phone number so I could find him at the airport.

I text him when I get there.

"It's Kennedy. I'm at the airport. Do you have a few minutes?"

"I just went through security. I'll turn around. Be right there."

And he is. He's out of breath like he was running. He has a big smile on his face that disappears when he sees me. I'm not smiling.

"Hi," I say.

"Thanks for coming."

I shrug.

"You wanted to see me before you left," I say.

"I did."

We both stand there awkwardly.

"What did you want?" I say in a cool voice.

"Your forgiveness," he says.

I squirm and look away.

"I know I have zero right to ask this of you," he say, "but I hope one day you can forgive me, Kennedy. I don't deserve it. I really don't. You and your mother didn't deserve any of it and I will live with that for the rest of my life. But I will always, always hold out hope that one day you can find it in your heart to forgive me."

"I don't know if I can forgive you," I say, exhaling loudly. "Part of me wants to. And part of me can't. I trusted you. You were supposed to be the one to protect me, Daddy. And you didn't. You were the one I needed to be protected from. You never hit me. But you hurt my mother and made me live in fear every day."

I'm fighting back tears with every ounce of my being.

I can tell he is, too.

"I understand, Kennedy. I really do. Really what I did is unforgivable. I have no right to ask your forgiveness. But I'm weak, so I do."

I don't answer. He looks down and swallows.

A voice over the loudspeaker announces that a flight to La Guardia is boarding. It must be his, because he looks up.

"I guess this is it then," I say.

He nods and says, "You have my number if you ever want to talk."

I fight back tears. My heart is breaking, but I nod. "I just might, you know."

He looks up and smiles. "So, you're telling me there's a chance?"

I smile back. It's a line from one of our favorite movies we watched together when I was younger, "Dumb & Dumber."

I don't say anything else, just turn and walk away.

I might just call him one day. My mom was right. Hating someone only hurts me. I can forgive someone without making what they did okay. I can forgive them for me.

I've forgiven Hunter a few times and I may end up forgiving him even more in the future. God knows, he's forgiven me during our time together.

I turn and stand watching my dad's back as he walks away. I take out my phone and type quickly before I can change my mind. Three simple words.

I forgive you.

He stops and pulls out his phone. I see his head bowed and then I see him stumble and reach for a nearby chair. He collapses in it and I see him lower his head. He's holding his head in his hands and his shoulders and entire body shake as he weeps.

I turn and walk away and know for certain that sometimes, just sometimes, forgiving someone for their benefit alone is also the right thing to do.

EPILOGUE

Six months without seeing Hunter nearly kills me. And him.

It helps us decide that no matter what stupid bullshit comes our way again, we will never let another person come between us again.

Josh Masters was convicted of assault and battery against Ava and also two counts of sexual assault and one count of attempted sexual assault. At the last minute, football player Chad and his dad took a plea deal and threw Josh under the bus, testifying against him.

He won't hurt anyone again for a long time. If ever. He will be required to register as a sex offender when he is released from prison. I don't have to think about him anymore.

But in the most shocking development of all, Ava and I are close.

During the time Hunter was gone, we met at least once a week. We often would go to dinner at a restaurant or even take walks on the beach. She still comes off a little bitchy to strangers, but I don't think she is mean spirited anymore. She told me that I'm the first friend she can really talk to. She didn't have an easy childhood and when I told her about mine, it somehow bonded us. We both had crappy dads and are still working all that shit out.

Now that Hunter is back, we still occasionally hang out with Dex and Devin. Coral and Dex broke up but they are still friends. They just thought it would be too hard to make a long-distance relationship work because after the first few weeks of school, a modeling scout approached Coral and offered her a deal she couldn't refuse.

She moved to New York and is pursuing a modeling career. She says she's going to chase it for a few years and then go back to college. Right now, she's jet setting around the world modeling and gracing fashion magazines. It's super cool.

Paige, the Brainiac of our friend group, is kicking butt at Stanford. We got together when she came home for Christmas. It was so great to see her. She has a really close knit group of new friends that are super smart like her. I'm so happy for her.

Dex and Devin have come into their own in the player department. They are dating different women every weekend and just having fun. They both say they aren't ready for a serious relationship. Dex seems much better and back to normal. I guess Coral said something to him and he went back to see a neurologist. They did some tests and put him in some therapy and he's better than ever.

Emma, my first friend in Los Angeles, has moved to Germany. We talk occasionally. She will always hold a special place in my heart for taking me in as the new girl and making me feel right at home.

I haven't heard from Dylan, but I did see a picture of him on TMZ with some gorgeous Spanish girl. The caption said she was a med student in Barcelona. The look on his face as he looked at her made me smile. I was tempted to message him about it, but figured it was best for me to be happy for him from afar.

Everyone is busy with their own lives, just like I knew would happen after high school, but it isn't as bittersweet as I once worried.

When I talk to my friends, it's just like we are back on Balboa Beach again. I know these friendships will last forever. What does make me sad is the friendships I had back in Brooklyn have faded. I once reached out to my ex, Ryan, and his girlfriend picked up and told me to never call him again. And I respect that.

And Sherie, my longest and closest friend, usually seems too busy to talk. But I don't take it personally. I wish her well. When I next go to New York to visit Coral, I'll see if she has time to go to lunch. That's all I can do at this point.

And then there is Hunter. The boy who captured my heart at Pacific High.

He's not perfect. And that's why I can truly love him. He has flaws and character defects. Just like me. And that's what finally has convinced both of us that what we share is more than just a high school romance.

We did decide to move in together to see how it goes. We found a cute apartment off campus that is basically someone's guest house. It is tiny but close to campus and has two bedrooms. We use one room as an office and have desks and our editing equipment set up there.

It's only been a month but so far so good. I took mostly general education classes the first semester so I could take a lot of the core film classes with Hunter. I've found we do really well working together as filmmakers.

Hunter's Fulbright that paid for him to film in Mexico was an insane adventure. I flew down there for a few days in the fall. We had armed guards the entire time. Hunter was so passionate about exposing the life that the children down there are forced to lead that I know his film is going to blow people away.

And I'm not the only one who thinks so. He showed it to the director of our department at school and she thinks that Hunter's film could win some serious awards. She's going to help him enter it into everything from the smallest local festival to Sundance and Cannes. I'm so excited for him.

He's so talented. We talk about carving out our careers in film together, producing and directing as a team.

We've been through a trial of fire. Our first year as a couple was full of more crazy drama than most people deal with in a lifetime. I want to say it's because it's L.A. but some of that insanity started for me back in Brooklyn with my dad.

That relationship is okay. It no longer makes me cry every time I think of him. He texts me every once in a while: maybe every month or so to say he loves me and is thinking of me. I usually just text back: love you too.

Because I do. I went to a few Alanon meetings with Oscar. He said it had helped him a few years ago when he was dating a recovering alcoholic. He thought since Hunter and my dad were both in AA, I might get something out of it.

And I did.

I learned that you can love a person and hate their behavior. I hate my dad's behavior and nothing will ever change that. But I do love him. And being able to admit that while not condoning what he did in the past has brought me a peace I never thought possible.

That peace and Hunter's love makes me realize that every day I have on this planet is a gift.

And that my job is to spread that peace and love in everything I do.

I'm up to the challenge.

The End

***

I hope you enjoyed this series. For more information on future books by Ashley Rose, please join her email newsletter here: https://www.subscribepage.com/ashleyrosebooks.

And also, you can email Rose at ashleyrosebooks@gmail.com if you'd like to see more books set at Pacific High or would prefer another series entirely.

***

This series dealt with some real life, difficult subjects that teenagers face. Please reach out if you or someone you know has experienced abuse. The CDC, Centers for Disease Control and Prevention, offers the following hotlines:

- Rape, Abuse and Incest National Network's (RAINN) National Sexual Assault Hotlineexternal icon
- Call 800.656.HOPE (4673) to be connected with a trained staff member from a sexual assault service provider in your area.

- Rape, Abuse and Incest National Network's (RAINN) National Sexual Assault Online Hotlineexternal icon
- Visit online.rainn.orgexternal icon to chat one-on-one with a trained counselor.
- In addition, here are some other options:
- National Teen Dating Abuse Helpline 866–331–9474 866–331–8453
- National Domestic Violence Hotline 800–799–SAFE (7233) 800–787–3224 TTY Rico and
- Rape, Abuse & Incest National Network (RAINN) Hotline 800–656–HOPE (4673)
- That's Not Cool www.thatsnotcool.com

According to the CDC, teen dating violence comes in many forms and can occur many ways, including the following:

- **Physical violence** - hurting or trying to hurt someone by hitting, kicking or any other form of violence.
- **Sexual violence** - forcing or trying to force someone into any type of sexual activity (even sexting) without consent.
- **Psychological aggression** - verbal and non-verbal abuse mentally or emotionally and/or trying to control someone else.
- **Stalking** - Repeated unwanted attention or interaction that "causes fear or concern for one's own safety or the safety of someone close to the victim."

PLEASE READ on for a sneak peek of Raven, a standalone young adult gritty mystery.

RAVEN

A halo of white light shines down from the sky illuminating the girl floating face down in the shallow water. The thumping of helicopter blades triggers a wave of goose bumps down my spine. I shrink back into my hiding spot on the beach even though the glowing circle cannot reach me. Waves spiral out from the body, making it bob unnaturally. I refuse to admit that *the body* is my friend Sadie.

She can't be dead. Dead is for old people. Not seventeen-year-olds.

A small boat creeps into the sphere of light. The night goes dark. The clatter of the helicopter blades fades and within a minute is gone. Two smaller, golden beams of light dance over the water. Dark silhouettes holding the flashlights drift back and forth on the boat. Low voices carry across the water.

"We got ourselves a floater. Been a few days."

"Grab that net."

"Rope's right over there."

"What's this?"

"Vicks. Ain't gonna smell pretty."

Floater. A few days. Ain't gonna smell pretty.

This must be a mistake. My cheeks feel icy even though the night air is hot.

Voices closer, on the shore this time, break the spell. Heart pounding, I scramble back through the bushes to the main walking path around the Lake of the Isles. I start toward the cop cars parked further down the jogging trail. I'd been headed that way until the beam of the helicopter's light lured me to the lakeshore.

Kicking up dust on the walking path, I wrap my arms around myself, darting glances at the bushes on each side of the path. I pick up my pace to a near jog.

As I get closer, the blue and red strobe lights flashing on the trees give me that same feeling I had in the bushes — that I'm dreaming and none of this is real. I stop at the mouth of the path. It's locked off with crime scene tape.

Behind it, several police cars and a big white hearse are parked on the side of the path. A few other clumps of people hang around nearby — a few joggers, but mainly teens. Two groups of them. Some I recognize from my school — Beth and her friends. I hang back in the shadows hoping nobody notices me.

Out on the lake, an engine sputters to life. At the sound, two men wearing black jumpsuits duck under the yellow tape, tugging a gurney behind them. The word "Medical Examiner" is printed on their backs in big, blazing white letters.

The humid air presses down on me and clogs my throat.

Outside the reach of flashing lights, the dark is filled with strange shapes and shadows. A rhythmic clicking from some animal seems close by, making me draw closer to the lights.

The image of my friend's small body glowing from the helicopter spotlight is burned into my memory. The back of her blond head. Hair fanned out in the water. Every once in a while, a sharp shoulder blade sticking out from a tank top bobbed to the surface. I squeeze my eyes tightly, hoping to rid myself of the image. Doing so only makes it worse, letting my mind run wild and imagine what I didn't see — her eyes, wide and unseeing, her body bloated and purplish with weeds wrapped around her neck.

My eyes snap open.

This can't be real. Sadie will come along that path from the lake any minute looking wet and tired and dirty, but alive.

I cast a quick glance at Beth and her friends. They're crying and hugging. Another group hovers near a tree talking to a cop, a little beyond the reach of the lights so it's hard to see their faces. They don't go to our high school, that's for sure. They look like those kids who hang out on the streets in Uptown with their pit bulls and cardboard signs begging for money. In the dim light, they all look the same — tattoos and leather and spikes and piercings and big black boots and Mohawks and dreadlocks. The orange glowing tips of their cigarettes leave streaks in the dark as they lift them to their mouths.

I use the hem of my shirt to wipe a glob of sweat dripping near my lip. I ran all the way from the bus stop on Lake Street.

I swat away a few mosquitos trying to feast on my bare legs. A big bushy mustached cop with a potbelly stands in front of the crime scene tape blocking the path to the lake. He clears his throat.

"Why don't you kids take off now?" He sounds gruff, but his eyes are kind. "You're not going to want to be here when they bring her up."

Beth gasps. But we all ignore the cop's warning.

I feel Beth's glare from a few feet away.

The night's humidity plasters her sleek black hair against her head. Beads of moisture rim her upper lip.

I have every right to be here. Same as her.

Sadie was *my* friend, too. Just not lately.

About an hour ago, Beth's mother had called mine, the phone ringing through our dark, silent house. Beth's dad was a cop. He often knew about anything bad that happened before anyone else. I'd picked up the phone in my room when I heard my mom gasp.

"They found Sadie's body. In the Lake of the Isles."

Body. Beth's mother's words echo in my ears.

On Friday, when someone at school said Sadie was missing, I figured she was at a friend's house. Maybe she got mad at her mom or something. We didn't talk anymore so I had no idea what was going on, but was sure it was a misunderstanding. She wasn't *missing*. It definitely never crossed my mind that she could be dead.

After my mom hung up, across the hall I could hear the muffled sounds of her crying. Sadie and I had spent every minute together from first grade to eighth. She'd spent so much time at my house that when it was time to do chores, my mother would call us both as one person: "Hazel and Sadie, come do the dishes."

I listened to my mom's choked sobs. I'd only heard my mom cry once before in my seventeen years — the time she stood over my hospital bed.

Within minutes of Beth's mom hanging up, I was gone, sneaking out of the house and on the next bus to Uptown. Now standing in the woods by the lake, I realize Beth must have snuck out, too. Although she would have driven her BMW instead of taking the bus like me. There is no way our moms would let us be here right now. I keep expecting mine to show up any second and drag me home. It's late — past midnight — and I'm sure my mom thinks I'm in bed asleep. Maybe she's up trying to figure out how to tell me about Sadie in the morning. I close my eyes and swallow the sour taste in my mouth.

A group of cops huddled nearby breaks apart. Some duck beneath the tape toward the water. One cop is still talking to that group of kids I don't know, the street kids. They listen and nod their heads, looking down at their big black boots. Did they find Sadie's body? Is that why they're here? It's hard to tell in the dark, but one guy wearing a newsboy cap looks familiar. I squint. A lot familiar. But from where?

Another police car drives down the narrow walking path, bushes and tree limbs screeching as they scratch its sides. This car doesn't have a cop decal on the door, but even from here I can see the glass separating the front seat from the back.

Everything happens at once. The bushes part and the two men wearing Medical Examiner jackets pass by me with a gurney containing a lumpy black tarp.

I shrink back. My throat feels like it's closing.

I catch snapshots, slow-motion images of everything around me:

A cop leading the street punks away to a squad car. Now I see there are three of them. They all get stuffed in the back of the unmarked car.

Beth shrieking and collapsing on the ground, her black hair drooping down over her face as she crouches on her hands and knees, her friends around her, patting her back.

A bloated, blue hand with chipped red nail polish slips out from under the tarp, off the side of the gurney, dangling, lifeless, bobbing along as it passes me. I blink. There is no hand. The bag is zipped tight.

I lean over and throw up, splashing some of my dinner onto my black Converse. I finish, bent over with my hands on my knees swallowing hard. I drag the tops of my sneakers through some leaves trying to scrape off the vomit. When I lift my head, I meet Beth's red and swollen eyes. She bites her lip and closes her eyes.

The men have loaded the gurney into the medical examiner's hearse. It leaves first. The other car follows. As the car passes, I see the profile of the guy in the newsboy cap in the backseat.

It's him.

READ MORE: My Book

Printed in Great Britain
by Amazon

22227477R00067